# FORGOTTEN BETROTHAL

Angeline felt she had to get away, make a new life for herself, become successful. After all, there would always be Marcus to call on if she ever needed help. Staid, sensible Marcus, who had once saved her from drowning — and how could she have forgotten what he'd promised her down by the breakwater all those years ago? Only when she had made a success of her life would she feel able to return to Viking Lodge — and Marcus?

EILEEN KNOWLES

# FORGOTTEN BETROTHAL

*Complete and Unabridged*

## LINFORD
*Leicester*

First Linford Edition
published 2000

British Library CIP Data

Knowles, Eileen
    Forgotten betrothal.—Large print ed.—
Linford romance library
1. Love stories
2. Large type books
I. Title
823.9'14 [F]

ISBN 0–7089–5731–5

Published by
F. A. Thorpe (Publishing)
Anstey, Leicestershire

Set by Words & Graphics Ltd.
Anstey, Leicestershire
Printed and bound in Great Britain by
T. J. International Ltd., Padstow, Cornwall

This book is printed on acid-free paper

# 1

The day had finally arrived. The moment she had eagerly awaited like a child anticipated Christmas. Freedom — it was hers at last. Angeline Frost strode purposefully out of the school gates and headed homewards, impatient to start the next phase of her life. She wouldn't have to put up with any more taunts and ribaldry from her classmates; she was finally free to do exactly as she pleased — or rather what her parents deemed suitable. Free to do what though? What would she really like to do?

Angeline frowned pensively, flicking her thick plait over her shoulder. School rules dictated she wore her hair restrained in such a manner. At least I will no longer have any need for that she reflected, and promptly removed the clip to release her long auburn tresses. It was her first symbol of independence she thought, and smiled wryly, it would be better still if she dare have it cut and styled. Imagine what her father would say if she had a short bob cut with a thick fringe!

*Young ladies are supposed to be dignified and gentle, and always have a good head of hair.* She'd heard the lecture so often she could recite it off by heart. *She ought to be extremely proud to have such glorious colouring — auburn was so attractive and unusual. Most people would give their eye teeth for such an asset.*

Angeline sighed. Why couldn't she be like other girls and have normal parents? She loved them both dearly, and would never do anything to cause them distress, but surely it was time she could make some decisions for herself. They had molly coddled her all her life, and now she wanted to rebel, but knew that she couldn't.

Carefully avoiding all the cracks as usual she walked along the pavement conjuring up career possibilities, none of which she would have any hope of pursuing. It would have to be something that didn't need great brain power. The only subjects she was any good at were mathematics and art, and then not exactly top of the class in either. The career's teacher hadn't held out much hope for her, and merely pointed her in the direction of child care or hairdressing, with painting as a hobby.

What did it matter anyway she muttered to herself, she wouldn't be allowed to take a job, or pursue any sort of career. Her parents had already decided that she need not go out to work. Their preference was for her to remain at home and become the housekeeper, now that her mother was finding it all too much to cope with. They maintained it would be good experience, since their objective was for Angeline to marry a nice sensible young man with prospects — like Marcus, and settle down to be a wife and mother.

Then they would feel they had fulfilled their duty.

Careers were for other girls, not someone of her position. Her father had been an acclaimed pianist before arthritis set in causing his enforced early retirement. *The Frost's were a family of repute*, her mother dinned into her almost daily, and she should acknowledge her position with gratitude. Angeline was grateful — they had been wonderful parents, but . . .

'Can I give you a lift, Angel?'

'Hi, Marcus. Thanks.' She had been so lost in thought that she hadn't noticed the sleek crimson sports car drawing up alongside. After first throwing her satchel and shoe bag into the rear compartment she scrambled into the passenger seat.

'Last day?' the driver said quirking an eyebrow in her direction before setting the car in gear and edging into the stream of traffic once more.

'Yes, isn't it great. I feel as if my life is just beginning, and the world

4

is out there waiting for me.' She stared down at her flat lace up shoes, grimacing with distaste. Those could be relegated to the dustbin forthwith along with her satchel. She glanced across at Marcus, he was smartly dressed as always looking fabulous, while she felt immature and awkward in her prim school uniform. 'Going somewhere important?' she asked wishing to sound more adult.

Weaving his way expertly through the traffic Marcus turned on to the Esplanade before replying. 'I've spent the morning wasting my time in court, and then had an extremely boring extended business lunch. Today has been a bit of a drag. You are the only bright spot in it so far,' he said flashing her a gleaming smile. 'I was on my way back to the office and remembered you would be leaving about now, so I thought you might appreciate a lift.'

She smiled her thanks. It was a thoughtful gesture on his part, but then that was typical of Marcus — discreetly attentive. She wondered what it must be like to have business lunches and to earn one's living liked he did. Marcus was highly successful — or so her father said, and it was to his credit that he had built the up the company to its present acclaimed status. He was something to be reckoned with in Scarcliff by all accounts.

He was her champion — her hero. He was quite good looking she thought, and she liked being seen in his company — it made the other girls jealous which was an added bonus. She liked the way his hair defied all attempts to restrain it. Lovely dark curls which gave him a boyish appearance, but she knew to her cost that he could be quite domineering when he chose. His eyes could change like the sea, from warm cornflower blue when he was happy to cold arctic grey when annoyed. Today they were sparkling cobalt and full of mischief.

Soon he was drawing up at the kerb outside her home — a large detached gentleman's residence set in extensive grounds on the outskirts of Scarcliff. Viking Lodge was an imposing house perched on an outcrop overlooking the town, with ancient woodland to the rear sheltering it from the west wind. It was an exclusive place with few neighbours to befriend or bother about.

'I'll call in to see your folks this weekend,' Marcus said, tweaking her hair as he dropped her off at the gate, 'so I'll see you then. I promised your dad I'd help him sort out some paperwork. Perhaps we can do something to celebrate your new found freedom.'

She thanked him politely, retrieved her belongings and walked sedately up the drive and round to the back door. It was Wednesday so her mother would be in the kitchen baking cheese scones and a jam sponge — the ritual never changed. Once in a while she wished they would consult her about some major event affecting their lives. She was after all a grown up now. She couldn't imagine her peers at school accepting such restrictions as she put up with.

'Hello dear, you're early,' her mother greeted her, looking flushed from the heat of the oven. 'Whatever happened to your hair?'

Angeline shook her head so that her hair fell forward over her face like a shaggy dog and grinned. 'I felt like liberating it. No more school thank goodness. Now I can get out of this ridiculous uniform and wear whatever I like, when I like.'

Her mother peered over her spectacles. 'Yes dear that will be nice to see you dressed more in keeping, although the uniform becomes you. I thought you liked green. With your hair colour it is most appropriate.'

Angeline picked up a warm scone and walked through into the hall niggled by the censure in her mother's voice. 'Where's Dad?' she called out belatedly, almost choking on a crumb in the process.

'In the library, resting. He's not been feeling too good today.'

Oh dear thought Angeline, wondering what to do about her school report. It wasn't as bad as she had been expecting, but on the other hand it wasn't exactly good either. She poked her head round the library door.

'Hi, Pops. Mum says you're not feeling too grand.'

Her father's eyes jerked open. 'Hello, Angie love. Is it that time already?' He peered at the clock on the mantelpiece, then consulted his pocket watch. 'Come to report in have you?'

'Not sure I should show you it right now,' Angeline said sauntering further into the room. 'Mum says not to upset you.'

'That bad is it?' He pulled a face and took the proffered envelope while searching for his spectacles. Angeline retrieved them from the floor and handed them to her father. 'It will be nice to have you at home more now,' he said. 'You don't need qualifications

9

for that, and there's plenty to keep you occupied in a house this size. Marcus agrees, he was saying the same thing only last week.'

Angeline shrugged her shoulders. 'I suppose so.'

She left him to read the report in peace and went up to her room, slumped down on the deep padded window seat and stared out of the window. How could she tell them that she wanted to leave — to leave Scarcliff and travel the world, and make something of herself. They had provided her with an excellent home for which she was truly grateful, but they weren't her true parents, and she felt beholden to them. She ought now to make her own way in the world, like Marcus had done. Why should the fact that she was a girl resign her to the inevitable?

She had visions of hitch-hiking to Australia, or working her passage to the West Indies — something exciting and adventurous. She had seen a program on television about younger people than herself setting off to explore the world, before settling down to what her folks would call normality. One day I will she said out loud. One day I will leave this town and only return when I have made a name for myself. I'll show them that Angeline Frost isn't such a dim wit as they make her out to be. I must be good at something.

She spotted the gardener busy cutting the back lawn. It was warm so he had removed his shirt — something her parents would surely disapprove of — especially her mother. She observed him covertly for a while as he pushed the old lawn mower backwards and forwards, making light work of it by all accounts. His muscles flexed with the exercise, and she thought what a fine specimen of the opposite sex he was — not that she had come into contact with many.

Medium length, rather straggly brown hair, blue eyes and impressive broad shoulders. He also had an extremely

11

sexy smile. That was what she first noticed about him. When he had introduced himself she had felt herself blushing, even before he said anything. She had admired him from a distance, ever since he replaced old Tom over a month ago. He was a definite improvement, and she wondered casually what he thought of her. Usually she had been in school uniform when they met and she had felt awkward and embarrassed, but now all that could change. In future she would be more out going, more emancipated she vowed, and there was no better time to start than the present.

On impulse she threw off her blouse and skirt and hunted through the wardrobe for her skimpiest dress. She found one which was only a year old and she had outgrown, but for some reason hadn't got round to throwing it out. It was the first dress she had been allowed to choose for herself which was probably why she had thought to keep it. Her mother had been going to accompany her on the shopping trip she remembered, but at the last minute didn't feel up to it and Angeline had to go alone.

She had needed the dress because they were attending a silver wedding party, and Angeline hadn't any outfit her mother deemed suitable. The dress she chose was a vivid blue with a swirling skirt of fine pleats, and it buttoned right down the front with tiny pearl buttons. She thought it divine, but her mother hadn't approved — too brash for her taste and too low a neckline, but it had been too late to change it thank goodness. She recalled Marcus said he liked it. He said it made her look more mature and very attractive, and Marcus didn't often dish out compliments — at least not in her direction.

Angeline pulled it on with a sigh of satisfaction. It felt tight across her chest now, so she left the top two buttons undone, and practised a provocative grin. When she caught sight of herself in the dressing table mirror and saw how short the dress was she nearly changed her mind. She had grown considerably during the past year — in all directions. Proudly lifting her chin and pulling back her shoulders as she had been taught to do in gym lessons, she reviewed her figure. She had read somewhere that girls should be proud of their bodies, especially their breasts, and hers were blossoming nicely.

She wished she didn't have freckles, but they seemed to go with her hair colouring. Picking up her brush she carefully arranged her hair into a pleasing style, clipping it so it fell over one shoulder like she had seen in a recent fashion magazine. Now she didn't look like a school girl she thought, and smiled at her reflection. Her hair was an eye-catching colour, she couldn't dispute that, but she felt certain it would look much better — more grown up if it was shorter. If only she could experiment with make-up, she would try to enhance her eyes so as to distract attention from her over large nose. Ah well, she sighed — one day.

Quickly she skipped to the door and hurried down the back stairs, hoping she wouldn't be too late and that Terry would still be around. She slowed as she approached the kitchen, and waited until she heard her mother go into the pantry, before passing through and out of the door unhindered. For a moment she thought he had already left and felt disappointed. She couldn't hear any noise, so she wandered slowly along the path to the summerhouse which was her favourite hideaway. She often took a book in there to read undisturbed, knowing her parents wouldn't approve of her choice of reading material.

The door stood open and she was about to enter when Terry surprised her. He was there already, lolling on the bench with a glass in his hand.

'Well, if it isn't Miss Angeline Frost, all grown up,' he drawled. 'I would hardly have recognised you.'

15

Angeline blushed. 'I'm sorry I didn't know you were in here.' She turned to go.

'Hey, don't leave on my account. I was taking five. Your mother brought me some lemonade. Want some?' He held out the glass, now half empty.

'No thank you,' she said sidling inside and taking a seat at the other end of the bench.

'Finished school have you?' he commented.

She nodded. 'Yes, thank goodness.'

'What are you going to do now then? Going on to College or University?'

'No, I'm afraid not,' she sighed. 'My folks want me to stay at home and look after them. They shouldn't be left alone, as neither of them is very well.'

Terry shrugged his shoulders. 'Tough,' he muttered. 'It's a big house to look after. Couldn't you afford a housekeeper?'

'Of course we could, but mother won't entertain having one about the place. She doesn't want strangers poking their noses into everything.'

She looked at him; his deeply tanned skin and smooth hair-free chest. That puzzled her. She had always thought men had hairy chests, but his was smooth as a billiard table. Marcus had hair on his chest, she'd seen it when they went swimming — a dark mat of short curls she remembered. Maybe that was because his ancestors came from the Mediterranean she thought. His dark swarthy appearance gave her that impression and some day she would ask him. She could hardly remember his parents, they'd died a long time ago, which was why he spent so much time at Viking Lodge she supposed.

The only clothing Terry wore were tight fitting jeans and old plimsolls. When he raised the glass to his lips she saw the way his chest muscles rippled so smoothly. They fascinated her, and at the same time she found them embarrassing. She knew she was about as tall as he was, but somehow she thought him a giant. His brash masculinity a shade over-powering. The convent school she had attended left her ill prepared for such feelings — such strange emotions — growing up type emotions.

'Want to give me a hand?' Terry asked, smiling brazenly as if he knew she had been admiring his physique.

'To do what?' she asked somewhat disdainfully.

'Thought you might like to assist with dead heading the roses or something. You must be bored to tears with housework, especially on a beautiful day like today.'

'Why should I?'

'Well, I only get paid for so many hours work,' he said getting to his feet. 'With your help more would get done in the time, and I also thought it might prove to be fun.'

'Fun?' she replied somewhat intrigued.

Taking her by the hand he laughed. 'Don't you know what fun is, my poor little Cinderella?'

She snatched her hand back. 'Of course I do, but I would hardly have thought . . . '

He grinned. 'Come, I'll show you.'

She half thought that he meant to take her in his arms and kiss her, so she backed away.

'I don't bite, you know,' he chuckled. 'I only meant to find you some gloves to wear. I wouldn't want you to spoil those dainty manicured finger nails. You're not exactly dressed for gardening, but if you stay on the path you shouldn't come to much harm.'

Angeline looked down at her hands conscious of her heart beating like a jungle drum, and knew her face would be beetroot red. She blushed far too readily, she always had done and it annoyed her intensely. She began to wish she had worn a T-shirt and jeans after all. She accepted the gloves which he unearthed and followed him as he headed for the rose beds. If she backed out now he would think she was snooty, like her classmates. Frigid Frosty they'd called her, and it was only after she looked the word up in the dictionary that she realised how insulting they were being.

Terry handed her a pair of secateurs and showed her where to make the cuts, then stood over her while she experiment with a few. She felt nervous with him standing so close, never having stood next to a near naked man before — except Marcus in his swimming trunks and he didn't count. When Terry appeared satisfied that she knew what she was doing he moved away to deal with the climbers which needed tying back to the wall.

Surprisingly, Angeline did find the work enjoyable. It was pleasant amongst the scented flowers, with nothing but the drone of bees to be heard, or the occasional seagull screaming overhead. She could let her thoughts wander at will, back to the old knotty problem of what she would really like to do with her life. Terry had assumed without question that she could do what was required once he'd shown her how. He hadn't called her an idiot or a numskull after her first fumbling attempt.

She kept looking across at him as he stretched out to locate hooks on the wall and looped the twine round them. Maybe staying at home wouldn't be so bad if she could help Terry. He came three afternoons a week, that much she already knew. His hours were the same as old Tom's used to be.

At five o'clock as they put away the tools and Terry slotted his arms into his shirt sleeves, he gravely thanked her for her assistance.

'I'll help you again,' she said eagerly. 'I think I might enjoy gardening. Old Tom never used to like me being around when he was working. He said I would be more trouble than I was worth.'

Terry gave her a lopsided grin. 'See you Friday then.'

She nodded and scampered back to the house, flushed and excited.

Each afternoon Terry came Angeline was there waiting near the tool shed. She prayed the sunny weather would continue, she would hate to have their meetings curtailed. Her parents didn't ask where she got to, they assumed she was quietly reading so she didn't enlighten them. Somehow she didn't think they would approve of her consorting with the hired help.

After two weeks she felt happier than she had done for ages. She helped trim the lawn edges and removed weeds from the borders. She steadied the ladder for Terry as he cut the privet hedge, and together they collected the cuttings for the compost. Best of all she liked the work in the greenhouse, watering the tomato plants and potting up seedlings and cuttings.

'What shall we do today?' she asked as soon as he arrived. It was overcast and she hoped it wouldn't rain. Today she wore a sunshine yellow T-shirt with beige slacks, and had tied her hair back with a ribbon. She hoped Terry liked it like that.

He pushed his bike up against the tool shed, and she sensed a look — not exactly of disapproval, but something.

'Something wrong?' she asked.

He shook his head and grinned. 'Nope. Only . . . well, do you realise how attractive you look I wonder?'

He strolled into the shed in his inimitable fashion, and Angeline followed cautiously.

'Do you really think I'm attractive?' she asked ingenuously. She knew that her nose was too large — her school friends had made her well aware of that. Nosy Angie was another nick name she'd had to put up with.

Terry's eyes crinkled in a smile as he turned to face her. 'Angie, if you were anyone else I would think you were fishing for compliments, but since it's you I have to say, that I have never met anyone so delightfully pretty. You have the most captivating nut brown eyes

I have ever seen. They are extremely expressive did you know? Sensuous sort of, hinting at a passionate nature.'

She smiled and breathed deeply, thrusting out her chest with pride, thrilled by his compliments.

He groaned and reached out for her. 'You are a temptress, distracting me from my work. Do realise that? Now I demand my reward. This is what happens when you look at me that way with those big beautiful eyes, so in future you'd better remember,' he chuckled mockingly.

Angeline's heart stopped beating. Immobile in his arms, and feeling the heat of his body squashed against hers, her breasts tingled. It felt sizzling hot in the gloomy tool shed, which had a strange characteristic smell of damp earth and creosote. All her senses were on intense alert as she looked up, her eyes wide with anticipation, and then she quickly closed them.

'What?' she breathed as his lips descended and she was transported to another world — a magical world of sunshine and roses and heavenly music. How had her hands come to rest on his waist she wondered? She couldn't recall doing it deliberately. She moved slightly fearing that she was about to overbalance which would send her toppling further towards him. In doing so he pulled her closer, and she could feel their bodies entwined from chest to thigh, hot and clammy, her fingers gripping his thin shirt.

'Oh,' she whispered as he gently released her. She couldn't go far though as he still held on to her, gazing down at her flushed face.

'Oh.' Her lips quivered and she nibbled them nervously. Had he felt the same way she had? Would it always be like that? The experience was all so new and incredibly wonderful.

He stared at her for a moment with a wry sexy smile, and then repeated the process, only this time he was more forceful and demanding. His tongue teasing and probing.

She gave herself wholeheartedly to his dominance, clutching at him with undisguised fervour. He felt strong and possessive as he clamped her tight against his chest, squeezing the breath out of her. Buttons on his shirt pressed hard into her over-heated skin, but she barely noticed the discomfort. It was her first real kiss and she was surprised by the softness of his lips.

When it was over and he released her she felt her knees buckling, and made a grab for the work bench. Her mind was in a whirl, all thoughts of where they were or what they were doing was immaterial, all she could think about was that Terry loved her. It had happened so fast that she was quite unprepared it. For some strange reason she had always thought she was in love with Marcus, and that eventually they would marry, although he had never said anything to that effect.

Terry in the mean time, whistling tunelessly, collected some tools from the far end of the shed, turned and handed her a hoe. 'Time to get some work done I think.' His voice was different — sort of husky and gruff. 'We'd better attack the vegetable plot in case it rains. I'd hate the management to find reason to sack me now. I am enjoying working here, especially with the perks it has to offer.'

Angeline stumbled outside and made for the back garden, her mind in total confusion. He sounded quite normal — as if nothing had happened! What had she expected — the earth to open up? It was only a kiss for heaven's sake she berated herself. Try to act grown up. Pretend that it was nothing new or special.

They worked steadily for nearly an hour, and then the rain came. At first it was nothing but a light shower, but then it grew heavier and they had to run for shelter — in the summer house.

'It won't last long,' Terry predicted, lounging lazily on the bench.

'Would you like some coffee?' Angeline

asked prowling round feeling distinctly nervous. 'I could go and make some if you like.' She didn't know how she should be reacting to his familiarity. Should she have slapped his face and stormed away when he tried to kiss her? But she had allowed him to kiss her — twice! What had she been thinking of? What would her classmates think now? What would they do in a similar situation? What would Marcus think of her behaviour if he ever found out?

Terry shook his head and patted the seat beside him. 'Come and sit down. Let's talk.'

'Talk?' she said, but sat down anyway a little distance from him.

He chuckled and slid along until he was right beside her. Slipping an arm round her waist he pulled her close.

'I thought you said talk,' she said shuffling uneasily, trying to put some space between them.

'I won't do anything you don't like,' he replied lightly. 'I thought you might like some instruction on what to expect now that you are a liberated woman — no longer a schoolgirl.'

She gulped. 'How do you mean?'

'How about coming out on a date with me?'

'A date? I couldn't.' She stared miserably at the floor and their wet footprints. 'My parents would never allow it.'

The only person they accepted as a suitable escort for her to go out alone with was Marcus. He had been a friend of the family since his father died and he had taken over the business. Her father was one of his oldest clients.

Terry's eyes glazed over and he shook his head. 'We'll have to make best use of my time here then won't we. You do like me don't you?'

'Oh yes,' she replied candidly. 'I know it may seem odd, but my parents . . .'

'How come they are so old?' he asked, easing her against his shoulder and smoothing out her hair. 'I guess you are only sixteen, and they look old enough to be your grandparents.'

She sank back against him with a sigh. She rather liked his masculine approach — confident and self assured. She was used to doing what people told her to do without question — at school and at home. She wasn't the rebellious type — except occasionally she rebelled against Marcus when he became too bossy. Not that it got her very far. Marcus — her adopted brother could quell her with a look.

'I'll soon be seventeen,' she volunteered, 'and if you promise never breath a word to anyone I'll tell you a secret,' she went on gravely.

'Promise. Cross my heart and hope to die.'

'They aren't my natural parents,' she admitted. 'They are in fact my aunt and uncle, but they have brought me up since I was a baby. My mother and my aunt were sisters. My natural mother died and my aunt and uncle took me in.'

'No father around?'

'No,' she whispered. 'I don't know what happened to him. They won't talk about him. It only gets them all upset if I ask.' She felt safe talking to Terry. She had never told anyone else about her dubious parentage, not even Marcus, too ashamed to admit that she might be illegitimate. 'You promise though, that you won't tell anyone.'

'What do you take me for?' Terry said bending over to kiss her forehead. 'Besides, what does it matter anyway? You are who you are. I for instance never knew my folks.'

His hand was creeping round so that it encompassed her left breast and she gulped. She liked what he was doing, but she had the feeling she should be outraged. She squirmed, but only succeeded in becoming more and more trapped. Slipping his hand under her T-shirt he laughed quietly as his fingers locked on to her nipple, and rubbed it gently through the thin lacy bra. She gasped at his audacity

31

but couldn't move — too mesmerised to do so. Marcus hadn't even kissed her, apart from a brotherly peck on the cheek, never mind what Terry was doing which was turning her bones to jelly. She moaned with pleasure.

'Like that do you?' he murmured and kissed her on the lips.

She turned and threw her arms round his neck and hung on tight. It was incredible. She felt wanton, yet wonderfully exhilarated. Growing up was a minefield of dilemmas to overcome, and she was so glad that Terry was prepared to show her what to expect.

★ ★ ★

That night Angeline went about in a daze. She was in love! Terry was the most wonderful, attractive man she could ever wish to meet. It was going to be so marvellous because he said he was moving into the room above the garage, so they would be able to meet more often. She didn't know who first made that suggestion but she was delighted at the prospect. Perhaps in time her parents would accept her fraternising with their employee, but for the moment it was a wonderful secret which she hugged to herself.

The garage was large and separate from the house — it had been stables once upon a time with a large roof space which had been converted into a useful room. Until recently the upstairs housed miscellaneous items of redundant household furniture she believed. She had never actually investigated because it had been kept locked and she didn't know where the key was kept. In the garage was her father's old Bentley car — his pride and joy which he would never drive again, but still refused to part with. Occasionally Marcus got it out and took them for a run in it, but not often.

Now apparently her father had agreed to adapt the room over the garage into a bedsit for Terry having learned that he had no where to live. It made sense he said because Terry could keep a general eye on the place and keep out intruders. Angeline envisaged sneaking over to see him, perhaps take him some home baking. She didn't want to discuss her new found relationship with anyone. She knew deep down that her parents wouldn't approve, so she wanted to put off the time when explanations were required. Fortunately her parents spent most of the evening watching television, oblivious to her dreamy state.

In bed she lay contemplating the future as Terry's wife. She couldn't wait for him to return after the weekend. She wished she could go out on a date with him, but now wasn't the time to broach the subject to her parents. Her mother was definitely under the weather. The doctor had been called in and he wanted her to go into hospital for tests, but her mother adamantly refused. She said she had never even visited anyone in hospital — she had a horror of such places ever since childhood. No amount of persuasion would get her to change her mind.

The doctor in the end told Angeline to see that her mother didn't over exert herself. She was to spend as much time as she could resting, preferably in bed. Angeline's immediate worry was that it would mean she couldn't meet Terry on Monday and felt guilty for such thoughts. As it happened her mother began having afternoon naps during which her father told Angeline to go out and get some fresh air. She couldn't be expected to remain indoors all the time. Angeline was relieved. She hurried to the tool shed on Monday afternoon just before two o'clock to find Terry already there.

'Hi,' she said, instantly blushing when she recalled their last encounter.

'That's what I like to see — devotion,' he joked. 'Missed me?'

'Yes . . . Oh no . . . it's just that . . . oh well, I didn't think I would be able to come at all. Mum's poorly.

I thought . . . anyway dad said to get some fresh air.'

'We'd best make a start then. The lawns need a cut, and the sooner we get started the more time we'll have for your lessons — in the summer house.' He said it teasingly, but Angeline knew what he meant and was as anxious as he was to get the work done.

The afternoon flew by. The weather was exceedingly hot — thundery she thought as they walked to the far end of the garden. By mutual agreement they decided to give the summerhouse a miss and get further from the house, so they could be away from prying eyes. It was a large plot, and some time ago her father had decided to let part of it grow wild to save on the maintenance. Here the grass was long and wild flowers bloomed quite freely. Angeline liked that part of the garden. She felt it was her own private territory since she was the only one who ever went there as far as she knew.

They walked as far as the misshapen

old apple tree which grew a little distance from the boundary wall. Here Terry flopped down in the shade, pulling Angeline down beside him. It was so peaceful and secluded. The eight foot high brick wall shielded them from their next door neighbour on one side and the wood on the other.

'Perfect,' Terry said stretching out lethargically, with hands behind his head pretending to sleep.

Angeline sat with knees hunched watching the bees pollinating the fox-gloves and wild roses. The only sound was of an airplane droning overhead and birds twittering in the wood. Shaking loose her hair, she picked some long grass and tickled Terry's face.

Quick as a flash he sat up, took her by the shoulders and pressed her down on the ground. She squealed with delight as he bent to kiss her. She was getting used to his kisses and enjoyed them very much.

'You're a tease, Angie,' he murmured, stroking her face with a remarkably light touch. She kissed the inside of his hand and smiled in what she hoped was a provocative manner.

Terry's hand continued down over her throat to land gently on her shoulder. She felt the straps of her suntop being pushed down to expose her breasts to the sunshine. She hoped to goodness nobody could see. It was exquisite torture — his hands kneading and massaging and when he bent to kiss her nipples she arched towards him. It was an instinctive reaction as pleasure rippled through her, and he assured her she was absolutely gorgeous and a first rate pupil. She gasped with alarm as his hand slid further down inside the waistband of her shorts. That felt too intimate, so she struggled to sit up, fidgeting with her straps.

'I think I ought to be going,' she muttered. 'Mum might be needing me.'

Terry rolled over and pretended to sleep again. 'It's OK. I understand. I told you I wouldn't do anything you were unhappy about. You're not ready that's all.'

'Do you love me?' she asked, watching him as he lay with closed eyes. She wanted to know what he was thinking. Could she trust him? She'd heard the other girls at school say 'boys only wanted one thing and when they got it that was the last you saw of them.' Surely that wasn't how Terry saw their situation was it?

'Love you?' He pondered for a few moments, screwing up his eyes as he peered at her silhouetted against the sunlight. 'It's too early to say. Would it make any difference anyway?'

She swallowed. She had been so sure that it was love — for both of them, and been prepared for the wrath of her parents when she informed them. It would have been worth it. Maybe it wasn't love as far as Terry was concerned she now realised to her horror. Her dreams cruelly shattered she grew angry. 'How do you mean? Of course it makes a difference.'

He sat up and aimlessly pulled at a clump of grass scattering the dry seeds. 'I am a simple gardener employed by your old man. You live in an enormous mansion.' He shrugged his shoulders to imply what more could he say.

Angeline wasn't sure what to make of his remarks but she was sadly disillusioned. 'You think I'm a prude don't you?' She slumped back against the tree sulkily.

'No I don't . . .'

'Angeline, where are you?' It was her father's voice, sounding extremely anxious and upset.

'Something's wrong.' Angeline quickly scampered to her feet. 'Coming,' she called out as she hurried through the rose garden, straightening her clothes as she ran. She could tell from the tone of his voice that it was something serious and she felt guilty for not being there when she was needed.

Her father's face was ashen and distraught.

'What's the matter, dad?' she asked,

fearing the worst, her voice little more than a whisper.

'It's your mother, love.' His hand shaking as he took hold of her arm. 'She's taken a turn for the worse. The doctor's with her now. I'm afraid . . . '

They went into the kitchen together and Angeline gently led her father into the library. She could see how distressed he was and wondered if he ought to have a drop of brandy. She didn't know what to say. One minute she had been so happy, and the next horribly guilty.

★ ★ ★

Angeline never knew how she got through the next few days. Her mother died three days later and her father slipped into a sort of dazed stupor. He became forgetful and strange, wandering about the house seeking something or someone, and kept muttering that he had killed her.

Angeline didn't know what to

41

do — how to cope. She tried telling him that it wasn't his fault, but he wouldn't listen. The doctor told her that it was temporary and it would pass, but she was horrified by the change in him.

★ ★ ★

After the funeral, when the few friends and relatives had departed and her father had gone to lie down, Angeline escaped into the garden. She needed a few moments to come to terms with what had happened. She had to some how accept her new responsibilities, but it wasn't easy. Marcus had been extremely helpful just as she had expected, but he couldn't spend all his time with them, he had a living to earn and other clients to assist. She wandered as far as the apple tree and sat down, but had only been there a few minutes when she heard someone approaching and knew it would be Terry.

'I thought I might find you here.'

'Oh?' She didn't look up or make any sign that he was welcome. After their last meeting she wasn't at all sure if she wanted to see him again. She had confused guilt-ridden feelings about the way she had behaved, and blamed Terry for a good part of it, since he was more worldly wise and shouldn't have taken advantage of her innocence.

'I came to offer my sincere condolences.' He stood looking sombre in a clean white shirt and black jeans, his hand resting on the bottom branch of the tree. 'I didn't like to attend the funeral. I thought it would be a family affair — no place for me.' He crouched down and placed a hand on her shoulder. 'I've moved in above the garage now, and saw you come down here. I thought perhaps I could help. I'd like to if I can, Angie. I've never been in your position, but I can imagine how you must be feeling.'

Tears sprang to her eyes. She

couldn't stop bursting into tears it would seem. He immediately dropped down and put his arms around her, rocking her gently and dabbing at her tears with a handkerchief. Soon they were kissing and hugging each other, and she found it so comforting. He could take her mind off the misery and guilt. In his arms she felt she could off-load all her problems. Their last difference of opinion was momentarily forgotten.

He was tantalisingly dominant, murmuring softly that he knew what she wanted — why she had come. His hands were everywhere, and at first she didn't mind. He was being so kind and sensitive. He understood how she felt, and she did need someone to share her grief. It was only when he began easing her skirt up over her hips that she began to have doubts about the wisdom of what was happening. He took no notice of her tentative protest. He didn't ask what she wanted, but over-rode her senses. It was only when he started to unzip his jeans that common sense prevailed. With a rush of blood she staggered to her feet, clutching her clothes about her.

'I have to go. I . . . I shouldn't be here. We shouldn't . . . '

★ ★ ★

After that she watched from her bedroom window as Terry worked about the garden. She wanted to go and apologise, but didn't feel that she could, or even ought to. She knew she had been right, and that she shouldn't have let their relationship progress to the extent she had. It all happened too quickly. She had been out of her depth, but she realised sadly that she was still in love with him.

# 2

The weather changed. It became much cooler and wetter. Angeline spent more time mooching about the house. She didn't feel she could spend long away from her father who was becoming more irrational each day. The housework was done in fits and spurts. Most of the rooms that were not used had the furniture shrouded in dust sheets, so they only received a cursory dusting from time to time.

She made short forays to the shops for essentials, but for the rest of the time she kept her father company. He seemed to have something on his mind which tormented him, and she tried to get him to talk about it. She felt certain he would feel much better once he had got whatever it was off his chest.

One evening they sat in the library — her father's favourite room, and he suddenly asked her if she ever thought about her mother. 'I mean your real mother,' he went on. 'Jeannie was so beautiful. You remind me very much of her. Her hair was the same colour as yours. It was a lovely flowing mane of auburn curls.'

'I wish I had known her,' Angeline said, wondering where the conversation was leading. She couldn't remember the last time he had mentioned her real parents.

'She loved you very much, Angie. You do realise that don't you? She thought you were a beautiful angel, even though she had so little time with you.'

'Yes,' she said. 'You did tell me, but it was such a long time ago.' She paused wondering if she could learn the truth at last without upsetting him. It had usually been her mother who had become annoyed whenever she broached the subject previously. 'What happened to my father?' she asked after a moments pause. 'Why didn't he take care of me?'

He looked at her rather strangely, and slowly began shaking his head from side to side frowning. 'But I am your father, love.' He cleared his throat and studied the fire. 'Didn't I ever tell you about Jeannie and me?'

She stared at him wide-eyed and speechless. She had never suspected he was her real father, even though she always called him pops.

He settled back in his chair rubbing a hand along his thigh. His eyes were bright and he had a relaxed smile on his face. He looked happy. For the first time since the funeral he looked content. She was bewildered by his statement, wondering how it could possibly be, and if perhaps he was having a brainstorm.

'Jeannie was so bright and full of life,' her father said, his voice soft with emotion. 'She was the younger sister — much younger than me of course, but it didn't seem to matter to either of us. Jeannie was fifteen years younger than her Sarah, and they were as different as chalk and cheese.

'Jeannie was abroad when I met and married Sarah so we didn't meet for three years or more. Then she turned up, quite out of the blue. Breezed into our lives like a wonderful breath of mountain air. I was bowled over by her vitality and compassion. We never meant it to happen, Jeannie and me — it was just one of those things. You won't tell your mother will you? She must never know that it's not my fault we couldn't have children. She believes it is you know.'

Angeline was confused, but then it dawned on her what he was getting at. 'Mum's dead,' she said quietly. 'She need never know.'

'Just so.' He paused for such a long time and Angeline waited desperately wanting to hear the full story. It sounded complicated.

'You and Jeannie . . . ' she urged after a while.

Her father looked at her with great

tenderness. 'Jeannie had hair the same colour as yours, and when she left it loose it reached her waist, just like yours. Sometimes she used to braid it with colourful ribbons, but I liked it best when it was free so that I could run my fingers through it. Her eyes were a stunning gentian blue, and she had the sweetest nature you can ever imagine. She couldn't bear to kill a spider even though she was terrified of them. She got me to catch them and put them outside.

'She was also very brave. She wouldn't let on to anyone that I was your father. She never told me — she obviously thought it would ruin all our lives if the truth ever came out, but I knew — I could tell. She was an artist you know — a very good one too. That's where you get your talent from.'

'I'd hardly call myself talented,' Angeline murmured wishing she had inherited his musical ability. She appeared to be tone deaf when it came to playing any musical instrument much to her parents' displeasure. 'Have we got any of her work?' she asked. 'I don't remember seeing any.'

'Yes, of course, but Sarah wouldn't give them house room. Jeannie was going to use the room over the garage as a workshop. That is where we stored all her canvases and other paraphernalia. Then one day Sarah and Jeannie had an almighty row. I don't know what it was all about, but the outcome was that Jeannie left — went away.

'She was such an independent free spirit yet could be quite determined when she set her mind on something. She didn't bother what anyone said about her, she went her own way and did what she wanted. She was always a happy soul though, and one could never be annoyed with her for long. One day she fell ill. She must have known she was dying, but all she told us was that she needed an operation. She asked us if we'd look after you until she was better — it was only going to be for a little while — so she said.

'You were only a few weeks old and as pretty as a picture. Her only concern was your welfare. In such a situation Sarah could hardly refuse her own sister. Sarah of course was delighted to have you, and promised faithfully to do her best and let bygones be bygones. The last words Jeannie said to us as she left was, *only the good die young*. I remember that as if it were yesterday, and we never saw her again.'

There were tears in her father's eyes as he recalled the past, and Angeline went to put her arms round his frail shoulders.

'I'm so glad you told me, pops. Is that what you've been worrying about?'

He smiled wanly. 'I keep seeing Jeannie whenever I look at you. She would have been immensely proud to see the way you've turned out. You're a good girl, Angeline. I hope you don't think too badly of me — or Jeannie.'

'Of course I don't,' she exclaimed. 'I love you, pops. You've been a wonderful father to me.'

'I think when I decided to open up the room over the garage for young Terry that it upset Sarah. I'm convinced that's what caused the final heart attack.'

'Oh no,' declared Angeline with exaggerated conviction. 'You mustn't talk like that. You mustn't blame yourself. The doctor said it could have happened anytime. Mum wasn't strong, and it was only through you looking after her so well that she lived as long as she did.'

Her father patted her hand. 'You're a good girl, Angeline. Maybe you're right. I hope so. I never wanted to do anything that your mother disapproved of. Sarah was a good woman. It was an aberration on my part — one moment of insanity, and I must take the full responsibility.'

Angeline thought he looked more like his old self after that, so she switched on the television thinking it might take his mind off his worries and they watched an old war film together. She herself hardly took in what it was all about though. Her thoughts were on what he had told her. She now knew the truth and she was relieved in a way. She was a Frost at any rate.

★ ★ ★

Marcus called often. He helped keep her spirits up and sat talking with her father, playing him at chess and letting him win she suspected. He helped them celebrate Christmas and birthdays which otherwise would have been particularly bleak times. He helped her trim the Christmas tree and escorted her to the carol service. Whenever he was needed Marcus was always there. There was even a mention of him moving in on a more permanent basis, but for the moment he was in the throes of selling his own house which was proving difficult.

* * *

He was there beside her, supporting her as always when eighteen months later, one April morning, Angeline again stood at the grave side in mourning, her father having died peacefully in his sleep. She was now all alone in the world to all intents and purposes. She had distant relatives but they only met up at such solemn occasions. She couldn't remember ever having attended a wedding or a christening. She would hardly recognise most of her relatives if they passed her in the street, but since most of them lived a long way away it was irrelevant.

There was only Marcus. Good old Marcus, what would she do without him? He had made all the funeral arrangements, but still treated her with reservation and respect — he always had done, but she wanted someone to hold her. She needed the comfort of a shoulder to cry on, but he was so formal.

Back at the house Angeline had arranged some light refreshments for the few relatives who felt obliged to return with her. They didn't stay long and finally there was only Marcus left. He seemed loath to leave her alone in the big empty house.

'Come, Angel. You have done your duty. Now it's time you thought about what you are going to do with the rest of your life.'

Angeline smiled wanly through the tears. 'I'll be all right thank you, Marcus. You've no need to worry about me. I'm not a child. I can take care of myself you know.'

'Yes, I know that you're an extremely capable young woman. These last couple of years you've coped magnificently, but why not come and stay with me, for a few days. You know that you are always welcome. I don't like to think of you alone at a time like this. You need some company. I'll get Fiona to stay too if would make you feel better. She could act as chaperone.'

Angeline appreciated his concern but didn't want to become a burden. Besides, Marcus she always thought of as being rather stuffy and serious. He went in for long winded discussions with her father and listened patiently to his advice. Occasionally he had accompanied her to a concert or other gathering, and always behaved in a brotherly way. He'd never attempted to kiss her the way Terry had, even though he wasn't much older than Terry.

'No, thank you all the same,' she said politely. 'I need time on my own to make some meaningful decisions. I have in mind to go away for a while.'

'That's a good idea. Have a holiday. It'll do you good.'

'I didn't mean a holiday,' she sighed shaking her head. 'I want to earn my own living.'

Marcus frowned. 'You know you've no need to . . . As executor of your father's will I can tell you that you have nothing to worry about on that score.'

'Yes, I do know, but for my own peace of mind I want to try.'

Marcus had been extremely helpful and a good friend all her life, and the last thing she wanted to do was to upset him. She was extremely grateful for all his assistance, she knew it was well meant, but it was now time she stood on her own two feet. She had to prove to herself and the people of Scarcliff that she could make something of her life. Besides she wasn't too keen on his girl friend, Fiona who was also his personal secretary. Fiona tended to make Angeline feel immature and a nuisance on the few occasions their paths crossed.

Fiona was an expert at everything it seemed. She was a fabulous cook, she could sew, bake, do shorthand and typing and was an extremely efficient secretary according to Marcus. She produced papers before he even asked for them, and could be relied upon to say the right thing to clients if he got delayed. It had probably been Fiona that had done the bulk of the organising for the funerals if the truth be known, but she gave Marcus the credit like a dutiful personal assistant that she was.

Closing the door having seen Marcus drive away Angeline wandered slowly into the kitchen and sat down. She needed to get away now more than ever. Ever since that horrible day — her seventeenth birthday no less. It should have been so wonderful. Her father — at Marcus's instigation most likely, had given her a brand new car — a super little mini, and arranged for her to take driving lessons. Angeline had been so ecstatic that she had run straight over to the garage to tell Terry all about it. She needed to tell someone and he was the only person she could think of — apart from Marcus.

She had stopped helping Terry in the garden, claiming her father needed her and she couldn't spare the time. She missed him though, and wondered if she was being naïve and immature by refusing his lovemaking. It still bothered her, because in her heart she sensed it was wrong, despite his assurance that he would do nothing to hurt her.

As soon as she entered the flat she knew it was a mistake. She sensed somehow that he wasn't alone before she saw the woman. The flat was only one room with the end partitioned off to make a kitchen area, and in the far corner was a small bathroom. The main door opened immediately on to the living quarters which included amongst other things a divan bed. Terry was in the middle of the floor pulling on jeans, while a woman with unkempt hair sat up in bed with the covers draped around her.

'Hi, Angie,' Terry said cheerfully. 'Anything I can do for you?' He didn't appear at all disconcerted by the predicament, but made no move to introduce his companion. Grinning roguishly, he picked his shirt off the chair and sauntered towards her as she stood in the doorway.

Why hadn't he locked the door she thought, grimly holding on to the door knob. Quickly appraising the situation she turned and fled without a word, embarrassed beyond belief and vowed that she would never ever go near him again. She never wanted to set foot in his apartment. She couldn't believe anything he told her, and clearly she was not his only girl friend as she had thought.

In fact it wasn't too difficult avoiding him. She soon deduced what hours he worked at the local supermarket where he was employed during the winter months, so she could easily avoid further confrontation. He did try to contact her, but she managed never to be available. When he had called at the back door she either pretended not to hear or persuaded her father to see him.

The summertime had been grim. She hadn't been able to go as often to the summer house or into the garden for fear of meeting him. On the few occasions they had seen each other she had scuttled away in the opposite direction. She had missed lazing in the long grass at the bottom of the garden, and instead had to drive out into the country with her sketch pad.

Now she reflected the sooner she put some miles between them the better she would like it. She didn't trust Terry any more, or rather her own emotions where he was concerned. She was confused and volatile. In her heart she longed for Terry. He would understand what she was going through and could commiserate with her, but she didn't know how to approach him. For too long she had kept her distance. Better to try to forget him and find someone new.

That night she started packing. But before that she entered her father's bedroom. In it was a trunk which she felt held the key to her very existence. She hadn't felt like snooping in it before, but now she knew she had to discover something about her mother's past. She had seen paintings her mother had done — some of them hung around the house now. They were landscapes — mainly of places abroad, but each had the location marked on the back, and she thought they were exceptionally good.

In the trunk were letters and photographs along with sketches and other memento, but nothing of consequence except perhaps a locket on a thin gold chain. She wasn't sure what she had expected, but there was nothing to reveal anything else about her natural mother. There were one or two photographs which she assumed were of her mother. She looked very attractive next to her more plain older sister Sarah. Shuffling the papers back into their envelopes she sighed. What did it matter anyway. She had to seek her own salvation, and she was determined to do it without the financial reward from the sale of the house. So many people seemed to think she had been born with a silver spoon in her mouth, and that she wasn't capable of earning a living. Well she was about to prove them wrong.

She would leave Scarcliff with a suitcase of clothes, her car and some jewellery which had been bequeathed to her, but nothing else apart from some paintings. During the past eighteen months she had spent a good deal of time drawing and painting — there had been little else to do apart from the housework. She felt she had improved considerably and thought perhaps one day she might be able to sell some of them. When she compared them to her mothers she felt reasonably pleased with her own effort. She had visions of becoming well known and her work sought after, but first she had to make the break with Scarcliff.

She had a reasonable sum of money in a bank account; pocket money she had saved at the dictate of her parents. No doubt Marcus would try to persuade her otherwise but she knew for her own self-respect she had to try to carve herself out a career. Only then would she be able to return and hold her head high in Scarcliff.

# 3

Angeline arrived in Mossdale, hot, tired and depressed. Now that she had freedom of choice she wasn't sure where she wanted to go or what she wanted to do. She had always thought the moment she was independent she would fly out to some exotic place abroad. Warm sun and tropical beaches beckoned, perhaps working in some posh hotel with fantastic wages. Now that she had the opportunity it all felt so daunting. She didn't feel at all well equipped with her few qualifications and insular upbringing.

Marcus had been sceptical about her leaving so soon, but Angeline couldn't wait to leave Scarcliff behind, even if it was only to the Lake District. Mossdale was only a two to three hour drive away, but at least it was somewhere familiar. She had spent some happy holidays there with her parents a few years back and liked the place, finding the scenery riveting. Mossdale she'd discovered was also where her real mother had been for a time before she died, so Angeline felt some affinity for the place. It was her birth place although she hadn't known until recently.

The town itself was in a secluded valley surrounded by smooth topped hills where sheep and fell-walkers roamed at will. It was an old market town with cobbled central square and numerous narrow side streets leading off, crammed with interesting boutiques and book shops. It was a tourist attraction in its own right, and a magnificent location for keen fell walkers. There were numerous walks within easy reach so it was extremely popular.

Angeline began to feel comforted by the familiar scene, and made her way to the hotel where they stayed previously. She pulled into the only vacant space in the car park and switched off the engine with a sigh of relief. She had arrived somewhere, and judging by the sign outside they had vacancies. She knew that she couldn't stay indefinitely in such an expensive establishment, it would be far to extravagant, but for the moment she wanted to get her bearings and have time to formulate a plan.

The last few days had been hectic — not that she had minded. She needed to keep busy to stop herself from thinking, and maybe talk herself out of making the break. It was a bold venture and she wondered if it was all going to be too much for her.

She'd left a set of her house keys with Marcus and he would tell Terry to keep an eye on the place. She wasn't sure how long she was going to be away but wanted the general maintenance to continue. Marcus agreed with her and to her surprise hadn't pressed her to put the house on the market, although she guessed he was thinking along those lines. Perhaps he was thinking about how long it was taking to sell his own property and realised now wasn't a good time.

He told her as he waved her off that if she had any problems — at any time she was to call him. Any time, day or night he would drop everything and come. At the time she had been somewhat disdainful of his even suggesting that she might need his assistance, but now she realised how alone she was. She thought she might ring him later and let him know that she had arrived safely at her destination. It would be nice to hear a familiar voice. She had no need to say where she was staying.

First and foremost though she had to get herself installed in the hotel, and then perhaps have a wander round the town before the shops closed. A walk might clear away the threatened headache, and she ought to make the most of the sunny weather. In that part of the country one could never tell when it would rain, and when it rained it came down in buckets.

Angeline was in luck. Within a week she had not only found herself a small flat but also a job. The flat was not very big — just a kitchenette, a small sitting room and a rather poky bedroom. The bathroom she had to share with another tenant, but since he was hardly ever there the landlord informed her, she should have no trouble getting along with him.

It wasn't quite what she had expected, but at least it was a place of her own and she could afford it. She decided that it would be worth living frugally for a time until she found out how easy it was to live on what she could earn. The job at a coffee bar was nothing very grand, but it was remunerative employment, and a start on her new way of life.

She was exceedingly nervous on her first day at the Coffee Bean, but fortunately since it was a Monday morning it was not very busy. She coped reasonably well, mainly clearing tables and washing up, but occasionally served customers and gradually found it became easier to do so. Her employer was a rather dour individual who spent most if his time in the back preparing the light snacks, although he appeared to have eyes in the back of his head.

Angeline shared the work serving the customers with an amiable Welsh girl who had started the previous week. Gemma was diminutive and chatty, and quite at home talking to the customers in her soft affable voice. She helped Angeline cope with their employer's brusque demands, brushing aside Angeline's nervousness and feelings of inadequacy.

'Take no notice of him,' Gemma whispered with a wry smile. 'For the wages he's paying he's lucky to have any staff at all. I certainly don't intend spending long here, but for the moment the hours suit me. My boy friend works round the corner at The Rose and Crown so it's quite convenient.'

On Friday, her first day off Angeline went to the hairdressers and had her hair cut. That was another milestone in her life. She couldn't recall the last time she had been to a hairdresser and didn't know what to expect. She had thought about asking Gemma's advice but resisted the temptation. This was something she had to do alone, and she didn't want to be talked out of it.

'Are you sure you want it so short?' the assistant enquired. 'It must have taken years to get it to this length.'

'Yes,' Angeline nodded gritting her teeth. 'Shoulder length to begin with I think,' revising her previous decision to have it extra short. At shoulder length she could still twist it into a French pleat or chignon so it would be adaptable. She hardly dare watch as the assistant snipped and snipped, and only hoped she knew what she was doing.

The final result truly amazed her.

The transformation made her feel giddy and light headed when saw to her delight that the new style suited her, framing her oval face to perfection. Her eyes looked larger and the wispy fringe partially hid her high forehead. Somehow her nose didn't look quite so significant either.

The assistant looked on with a benign smile as Angeline stared at the new, unfamiliar image and then down at the carpet of auburn locks that littered the floor.

'You have beautiful hair,' the assistant said recognising Angeline's nervousness. 'It's been a pleasure to style it for you. I feel quite envious of the colour, and I'm sure you'll find it easy to cope with now once you get used to it.'

Angeline walked back to her flat with a bounce in her step, involuntarily looking in all the shop windows at her new appearance. She felt older, having finally discarded her schoolgirl image with absolutely no regrets. She was beginning to believe in herself, so she held her head high clearly pleased with her new personality.

'You live here?' a voice behind her enquired. Angeline, busy fishing in her handbag for the flat key, hadn't noticed the man approaching. She had been too busy with her thoughts, wondering if Marcus would approve of her new hair style. Turning in surprise she found a tall, rangy stranger had followed her into the flats' entrance.

'Yes, I do, as a matter of fact,' she stuttered, guessing that he must be the other tenant — the one she shared a bathroom with. 'Do . . . do you?'

'Things are looking up,' came the chirpy reply. 'The name's Russell Watson. The last occupant of your rooms was an old dragon of a woman. Nagged me continually, usually about the time I spent in the bathroom, yet she was in there far more than I. And she didn't always wash the bath out after her either.'

'Oh,' Angeline said dropping her key, feeling flustered by the good looking individual who was clearly taking a full inventory of her vital statistics. She had seen the same look on the faces of some of the customers at the coffee bar. 'I'm Angeline Frost. I only moved in a few days ago.'

'Nice to meet you, Angeline. Mighty pretty name to describe a beautiful young woman. What does everyone call you? Angel or Angie?'

'Angie generally.' She blushed. 'Angeline is a bit of a mouthful, and Angel is hardly appropriate.'

He laughed — a deep throated laugh which caused her to smile wryly.

'Well now, Angie, how about we cement our new relationship with a spot of food. I'm starving and I've not a bean in the place. I'm not here often enough to keep much in the larder.'

Angeline blinked with the suddenness of his invitation. She was only going to scramble some eggs which she had just bought. 'That would be nice,' she found herself saying. 'Thank you. I must put this shopping away first though.'

Russell was by now picking up his mail which was left on the entrance table. 'Great. Give me ten minutes to see what's in this lot and to freshen up. I'll knock on your door when I'm ready shall I? I hope I'm not treading on anyone's toes?' he said as an after thought.

Angeline shook her head and floated into her flat. She sat down in front of the dressing table mirror hardly able to contain her happiness at the way things were turning out. She stared at her reflection, pleased with herself and her new hairdo. She had a place to stay, a job and now a friend — a man friend.

Russell was nothing like Terry. He was older for a start. He must be well over six foot tall, with dark brown hair and grey green eyes. She noticed he had a weather-beaten appearance as if he spent a good deal of time outdoors and wondered what he did for a living. She didn't recall the landlord telling her. Angeline barely had time to wash her face and comb her hair before he was knocking at her door.

'Like to go somewhere local, or do you fancy a run out to a place I know? It's not far but the food's superb and worth the trip.'

'I don't mind. You choose. I'll be happy either way.'

'Let's drive then. My car's still outside. I wish all women were as easy to please,' he chuckled leading her to an old-ish two seater sports car parked neatly outside the next door property.

'Bessie here may look ancient but she's never let me down yet,' he informed her quite seriously, and as he switched on the engine sprang to life with a harsh growl.

Soon they were tootling through narrow country lanes that twisted and turned along the valley bottom. Eventually they came out beside a small lake and Russell drove into a pub car park at the far end of it. The pub didn't look very busy, there were only two other cars parked outside.

'It doesn't look much I admit, but if you don't agree that it's the best food you've ever tasted then I'll eat my hat.' Russell promptly pulled on an American type baseball cap which had been residing between the seats.

She laughed at the prospect and struggled to disentangle herself from the seat belt. 'It looks pretty indigestible to me, so I hope you're right.'

The pub was very old and run by an elderly couple who greeted Russell with obvious pleasure. He in turn introduced Angeline and they made her welcome. Once settled in the bar with liquid refreshments Russell asked her how long she had been in Mossdale.

'Not long. I came here with my parents for a holiday a few years back, and rather liked the place so decided to come and seek work here.'

'Good for you. So where are you working?'

She frowned. 'I've got a job at the Coffee Bean on the corner for the moment ... that is until I find something more appropriate.' It sounded so uninteresting and mundane.

'You have to start somewhere.' Russell smiled sympathetically. 'Better than being on the dole. Where do you come from originally?'

'Scarcliff, do you know it?'

'I know of it,' he replied. 'Can't say I've ever been there. It must have been quite an undertaking to leave home at your age.'

Their meal arrived and for a while little was said. Russell didn't initiate a conversation so Angeline followed his example and remained silent. She wondered what Marcus would say if he knew she had got into a car with a complete stranger — not that she viewed Russell as a stranger when he lived at the same address. Somehow she summed him up as completely reliable and honest, even though she knew little about him.

'Fancy a sweet?' he asked when they had both eaten everything put in front of them. The helpings had been gigantic.

Angeline rolled her eyes. 'I couldn't eat another thing. That was superb.'

'I told you,' he grinned as the landlady arrived to clear away the plates. 'Another satisfied customer. Your reputation is spreading.'

The landlady looked embarrassingly pleased.

Russell ordered two cups of coffee and then they began discussing the work prospects in Mossdale. How it happened, she wasn't sure later, but she ended up telling him all about the death of her parents, and gave him a brief resume of her life story. He was a pleasant companion, and as they entered the flats again she thanked him generously for a lovely time.

'My pleasure,' he said. 'I suppose you will be working tomorrow?'

She nodded. 'I'm afraid so,' and looked at him questioningly.

'I was going to suggest you join me on a walk. Obviously if you haven't been here long you haven't had time to do much fell walking.'

'No,' she agreed, 'but I would love to one day. I've bought myself some boots and waterproof clothing.'

'Perhaps next time I'm here we could arrange something.'

'That would be great,' she said beaming broadly.

★ ★ ★

During the following week Angeline kept hoping that Russell would be back at the weekend so they could go out walking as he suggested. She often looked up at the mountain tops and wondered what it must be like up there. She knew there were well defined paths, but so far she hadn't had the courage to try them.

Unfortunately Russell didn't arrive. Not Friday, not Saturday. She was disappointed since she had been given Saturday off and it would have been an ideal day for an excursion. When she saw their landlord she casually asked him if he knew where Mr. Watson lived during the week and what he did for a living.

'Oh, so you've met Mr. Watson have you? Good chap, pays his rent on time and I hardly ever see him. An ideal tenant so I don't ask questions. What he does is his business and I keep my nose out of it.'

Feeling snubbed Angeline retired to her room. A whole day with nothing to do and the flat felt claustrophobic. The hills were clouded in mist so she got out her pad and decided to walk down to the river, hoping to find something suitable to sketch. She spent a couple of hours on the river bank and produced several rough sketches before wandering back into the town to browse around the shops.

It was market day and she was attracted to the numerous stalls set up in the square. She purchased several items which would brighten up her flat, and on the way back she spotted a picture gallery which she hadn't seen before. She was so well laden that she didn't feel like going in so made a mental note to pay it a visit another day.

All week Angeline prayed that Russell would arrive the next weekend. She was to have Sunday off. He arrived late Friday night. Angeline was already in bed but recognised the rasping exhaust note his car made as he drew up outside. She went to work the next morning joyfully, and towards lunch time he strolled into the coffee bar.

'Hi,' he said as she hurried to serve him before Gemma did. 'Just a coffee and a ham sandwich.'

'Certainly, sir,' she replied flashing him a brilliant smile. When she returned he was reading the morning newspaper. 'It's my day off tomorrow, isn't that great,' she told him.

His eyebrows lifted marginally.

'I thought . . . if you remember . . . ' she stammered.

'Of course. I'm sorry I was miles

away. Where did you fancy going?'

'I don't know. What ever you think suitable.' She blushed wondering if he would think her pushy, and maybe he hadn't intended going fell walking. 'I'm sorry, I shouldn't . . . it doesn't matter . . . ' She started to walk away.

He got up and caught her arm. 'I'm sorry, Angie. I was a bit distracted. Of course we'll go out — somewhere tomorrow, but what time do you finish today?'

'Six o'clock, why?'

He gave her a lop-sided smile. 'I'm at a loose end so why not spend the evening together?'

'I'd like that,' she replied shyly and hurried back to the counter to serve another customer, ignoring Gemma's mischievous questioning look as best she could.

★ ★ ★

Russell knocked on her door at seven as arranged. She was taken aback at the sight of him in a formal suit. He looked different — older somehow, but quite handsome.

'I thought we'd stay in Mossdale,' he said lounging against the door opening. 'There's a charming little Italian restaurant I know, in walking distance. OK? I don't drink if I'm driving and tonight I feel as if I could do with one.'

'Sounds super.' She picked up her cardigan and joined him, wondering if she could tell him that she was only eighteen and didn't drink much. They walked towards the town centre, the evening balmy with only a slight breeze disturbing the leaves on the trees. She was speculating on how old Russell was. He had an air of authority which usually came with age, and he had grey hair showing at the sideburns she noticed.

'You're quiet,' he murmured. 'Most unusually so for a female I find. I guess that was your upbringing. Are you enjoying yourself, Angie, now that you've broken free?'

'Yes,' she said thoughtfully. 'On the whole I am happy with my life, but I wish I could find something more rewarding to do. The coffee bar was a stop gap.'

'What would you like to do? Where do your talents lie?'

'I'm not sure if I have any,' she replied, by which time they had arrived outside the restaurant.

Once seated at a table and they had selected from the extensive menu Russell prompted her about her aspirations. He was like a dog with a bone, wanting to know why she was wasting her time doing such a servile job.

'Every one has talent. In some it lies dormant and requires something to kick start it. I can't believe you are a complete duffer.'

'Well . . . art is my strongest subject. I take after my mother I suppose,' and she carried on to tell him about her natural mother.

He listened intently, nodding his

approval. 'Great. You couldn't be in a better place than Mossdale to try your hand.'

Feeling encouraged she told him about her own work. 'I have made a start. I did some sketches down by the river, and though I say it myself I'm quite pleased with them. I did a few rough drawings of people I saw and wondered if I could interest the tourists along those lines.'

'That's better. Now you're thinking positively. I should think the visitors to Mossdale would be entranced to have a portrait done by you. Can I see what you've done so far?'

'Of course if you like. I'd value your opinion.'

It was a pleasant leisurely meal, and afterwards they strolled back to the flats discussing the walk they proposed completing next day. As they entered the front door the landlord accosted them wanting a word with Russell so Angeline went to her room, after thanking him for a lovely meal. She said with a grin that she would show him her etchings the next day if he liked.

* * *

The day turned out to be warm and sunny. Angeline packed the sandwiches, fruit and tins of cola as agreed, and also added her sketch pad. She was ready in plenty of time and sat debating whether she needed to take a jumper.

Russell arrived complete with maps, and wished her a cheery hello. 'It's going to be hot,' he remarked, 'but don't forget a sweater for on the top. It can get quite a bit cooler up there.'

Angeline felt awkward walking down the street in her hiking boots. It was the middle of summer, and back in Scarcliff one wouldn't dream of wearing such clompy footwear, but it was what everyone else seemed to be wearing. The sun felt warm on her bare arms and she was relieved that she had thought to put on the sun block since she tended to burn easily.

Russell was in thoughtful mood so they walked in silence. He led her along a path away from the town centre. The path meandered through a wood before the climb proper began. It was cooler under the trees but Russell set a steady pace which at times Angeline found difficult to keep up with. She stopped from time to time to admire the view and catch her breath, realising how unfit she was. Russell wasn't even breathing heavily. It was almost a stroll so far for him, and yet she was finding it hard going.

Angeline enjoyed the walk even though Russell had at times to coax, bully and even berate her lethargy. He was in a strange mood for most of the day. Often quiet, and she wondered at times if he forgot she was with him.

They arrived back in Mossdale in the early evening, tired but exhilarated — at least she was. She had actually stood on the top of the mountain which overlooked Mossdale. She saw the mountain daily — sometimes it was shrouded in mist, but today it had been as clear as a bell. The views were stupendous, and now she knew that she wanted to capture them on canvas.

'Would you . . . can I prepare us a meal? What I mean is . . . '

He grinned and squeezed her arm. 'I'd like that. But first you'd better soak in the bath. Your muscles have taken a hammering today, and by tomorrow you will be wondering if the agony was all worth it.'

She laughed. 'I'm sure it was. I've thoroughly enjoyed it and I've decided that I am going to start painting in earnest. I can't wait.'

★ ★ ★

Angeline prepared the meal. She'd given it a lot of thought the night before, wanting it to be in the way of a thank you for his kindness. He'd taken her out for two meals and wouldn't let her pay her share on either occasion. The sitting room was only small but it was better to eat there she thought and use trays than cramped up in the kitchenette. Russell arrived and she gave him her sketches to look through while she finished preparing the rice.

After a while he appeared at the kitchen doorway waving the drawings. 'These are dammed good, young lady. How can you say you have no talent?'

'Do you really think so?' She blushed with pleasure.

'If you don't believe me, go and take a look at that fancy gallery in the town centre. I wandered round there the other week and there was nothing as good as these, and they are charging the earth.'

During the meal Angeline told him what she intended doing and he agreed with her wholeheartedly. She had bought a bottle of wine to have with their meal — a wine which Marcus preferred so she hoped it would be satisfactory. Russell had most of it, but Angeline did manage the odd glass, and it helped bolster her confidence no end. Afterwards she sat beside him on the settee enthusing over her new ideas.

'I'd really like to run my own business — a shop or gallery where I can sell my own work — as well as some other paintings which I have. There may even be local artists who'd welcome having their work on display. I only hope that I wouldn't have too much competition.'

'May I say what a remarkable young woman you are, Angie,' Russell said as the clock struck ten and he prepared to take his leave. 'I wish you all the luck in the world with your aspirations. Take my advice and have a go. What have you got to lose? You'll regret it later if you don't take the plunge while you're young and enthusiastic.'

He put a hand on her thigh and leant over to kiss her cheek — a brotherly peck that was all. She smiled up at him, her face animated with wine heated blood and promptly threw her arms round his neck and kissed him full on the mouth.

'Oh, Angie,' he sighed hugging her close. 'My dear girl. If only . . . You know you are asking for trouble if you go around flashing those beautiful brown eyes at the guys like that.'

She tried to break away feeling rather foolish. 'I'm sorry . . . I shouldn't have . . .'

He got to his feet looking a shade embarrassed and strolled to the window. 'It's not what you think, Angie.' Glancing down at his car he then turned to face her. 'I find you an extremely attractive young woman, don't get me wrong, but I wouldn't want you to do something which you would later regret. I know what I'm talking about. I'm too old for you . . .'

'Oh, but you're . . .'

'I'm also married, sweetheart.'

She blanched. That was something she hadn't thought of.

'My wife and I have been going through a tricky time recently, which is why I took rooms here — to get right away and have time to think things through. I'm sorry if this comes as a surprise. I didn't mean to deceive you.'

'No, it's all right . . . you didn't. I wasn't thinking. I have enjoyed every moment we've spent together, and I wanted to repay you.'

She hung her head with embarrassment.

He walked over and took her in his arms. Tilting her head up to face him. 'Believe me, my dear, one day you will meet some nice young man of your own age and you'll be glad that you didn't devalue yourself, and he'll be one hell of a lucky guy. You make sure that he's worthy of you.' With a brief kiss on the forehead he left.

★ ★ ★

Angeline hardly slept. It was daylight before she dropped into a troubled

94

sleep to dream dramatic, sometimes passionate dreams. She woke feeling dreadful. Her head felt woolly and her mouth like sand paper. One glance at the clock and she knew that she was going to be late for work. For a split second she lay back and closed her eyes wondering why she was bothering. Why was she slaving away for a pittance, especially for someone who didn't appreciate her, but then she sighed. It had been the only job she could find since she had no qualifications, so she was determined to do her best while ever she worked there.

When she came to get out of bed things got instantly much worse. She found she could hardly move. Every muscle ached. It was with a supreme effort she managed to walk — or rather stagger stiff legged the short distance to the bathroom. She was so conscious of her mobility problem that it was some time before she realised something was wrong, something missing. Her mind wasn't functioning properly. Then she realised what it was — Russell's shaving gear and towel, his drip dry shirt he'd hung over the bath — everything had gone. She didn't need to look out of the window to know that his car would be missing also.

Stumbling back to her room she noticed his door slightly ajar and instinctively pushed it open. He'd left! Gone. There was nothing of his in the room. She couldn't believe what she was seeing, and it was only as she got back into her own flat that she noticed the envelope on the floor.

*Dear Angie,*

*Thank you for everything. I have enjoyed your company more that you will ever know. Now that my divorce is going through I have decided to join a friend in France. He wants me to go part share in a vineyard. I'll let you have the address so that if you are ever in my part of the world I hope you will drop in.*

*Good luck with your new venture,*

*and the next time I'm in Mossdale
I will look out for the elegant Frost
Gallery which I'm sure will be an
immediate success.*

*Your friend still I hope,*
*Russell*

By the time Angeline had read the
letter, had a cry and got herself ready
for work she was already late. The
walk to the coffee bar was excruciating,
but gradually the muscles relaxed and
became more usable. By the time
she arrived outside the Coffee Bean
she was congratulating herself on her
speedy recovery, noting that she was
only twenty minutes late, and it was
very early morning so shouldn't be a
problem.

'What time do you call this?' her
employer admonished her as soon as
she walked in the door. 'I thought
you said you were conscientious? I
don't call being half an hour late
being conscientious.'

'I'm sorry,' she murmured flinching

under his tirade. 'I don't feel too good.'

He looked at her sternly. 'Been out in the sun too much?' he snapped. 'Had a late night last night with the boy friend? I don't know what the youth of today are coming to.'

'No,' she sighed, but the way he was looking at her incensed her. Suddenly something welled up inside. She didn't have to take his bad temper and his offensive remarks. She didn't need the job. Gemma was right he was a mean old scrooge with no regard for his staff or even his customers come to that. He might at least have asked for an explanation before reprimanding her. Taking a deep breath she stared him full in the face. 'No, it was nothing like that. I . . . I wish to hand in my notice.'

To which he threw up his hands in despair and snarled that for what good she was she might as well leave immediately. Angeline turned and walked out without another word.

She had no regrets either except she felt sorry for Gemma who would no doubt bear the brunt of his bad temper for the rest of the day. She was glad now that she had made the decision. She had told Russell that she was going to open a gallery and that was exactly what she was going to do. It hadn't just been the wine talking the previous night, she really did want to make a success as an artist.

On her way back to the flat she made a detour to look in the window of the gallery Russell mentioned, and she had to agree there was nothing there that she felt she couldn't have done better. That gave her hope, so she paid the estate agents a visit to discover what property they had to let. Armed with the lists she settled down with a cup of coffee to see what appealed within her limited budget.

She was still loath to dip into her savings too deeply, so a shop that was already decorated and ready to walk into would be the most suitable.

Finally she eliminated several as totally unsuitable either because of their size or situation, but it still left about half a dozen for her to visit. She wished Russell was still there to advise her, or even Marcus. Should she ring Marcus and ask his advice? No better see what was on offer first and then perhaps ring him tonight. Dear Marcus, he'd said she only had to ring — any time.

Feeling better now that she had something positive to concentrate on she set out again. Her limbs were finally accepting movement without too much protest. Mossdale was relatively quiet and she found most of the properties without too much trouble. Several were not quite what she was looking for, and some certainly could be crossed off her list as totally unsuitable.

She had almost given up hope of finding anywhere that she could afford and was suitable, when she came to the last but one of those for which she had details. It took some finding, but when she did locate it down a side street off the market square she knew instantly that it was ideal. It was rather more money than she wanted to pay, but then she noticed that it had rooms upstairs used as living accommodation by the previous tenants.

Quickly she retraced her steps and obtained the keys from the agents. She was nervously excited as she let herself in, trying not to get her hopes up too high. The shop part was reasonably spacious and already contained some fittings, but the walls she noted would need a fresh coat of paint. There was a tiny room at the back which she guessed would be used as a store room with a window looking out on to a yard — a suitable place to park her car.

Upstairs was a small galley kitchen, a tiny bathroom, one small bedroom, and finally a medium sized sitting room. It was carpeted throughout — albeit with poor quality carpet, but what impressed Angeline most was the superb view from the sitting room window. She was almost dancing with delight having learned that she could take immediate occupancy. It was perfect. She knew she wouldn't find anything better, so she returned to the estate agents office chewing over in her mind what she would need to purchase to make the place liveable. Mentally reviewing her finances she felt certain that she could manage without having to ask Marcus for a loan.

She had to tell someone about her new venture and since she had no phone number for Russell or Terry it had to be Marcus. He sounded as stuffy as ever she thought, but she was past caring as she gleefully explained what she was going to do.

'I'm delighted for you, Angel, and I hope it is a great success. Are you sure you wouldn't like me to come over and help in some way. Check out the agreements and so on, give it the once over?'

'No, thanks all the same. I didn't mean to disturb you, but I wanted to tell someone and you were the first person I thought of.'

There was a pause before Marcus answered, his voice softer and most endearing. 'I'm honoured, Angel and pleased that you are sounding so much better. Scarcliff isn't the same without you, but I do understand how you feel. Do keep in touch and if there is ever anything I can do, don't forget, I'm always here for you.'

As she put the phone down she wasn't sure if she had heard correctly. Had he called her sweetheart? It was most unlike him to be emotional or to get carried away. Dear Marcus, he was a treasure.

# 4

'I'm afraid we're not opening until Monday.'

Angeline wasn't exactly dressed for greeting potential customers. It had taken several days of hard graft to get the shop into anything like a suitable condition but it was very nearly ready. The fresh paint smell still lingered, but at least it was light, bright and airy. Onions sliced in half said to combat the paint smell didn't seem to be working, but it had been a tip given her by the boutique owner next door so she felt obliged to try it.

A workman was fixing a sun blind in the window, which was something Angeline didn't feel competent to tackle on her own, so she thought it ought to be fairly obvious that she wasn't open for business. Boxes were strewn about the middle of the floor, and she was about to start hanging paintings round the newly decorated walls.

The man had wandered into the shop, nonchalantly looking around. He was young, good looking with an open friendly face, and for some reason he seemed vaguely familiar. He was smartly dressed in a fashionable grey pin stripe suit relieved by a rather garish pink shirt and fancy tie, so evidently wasn't the usual tourist out browsing.

Angeline had been rummaging through some boxes recently delivered, checking the contents. Now she swept hair out of her eyes and grimaced at the sight of paint on her hands.

'I heard you were setting up, and since we are in the same line of business I thought I'd look in,' the man announced, smiling at her look of wariness. He entered further into the shop carefully avoiding the newly painted surfaces and approached Angeline, handing her his business card.

'It's all right,' she said with a smile.

'The paint is dry.' Then, glancing at the card, it dawned on her who her visitor was. 'You don't mind my setting up in opposition?' Putting the card on top of one of the boxes she wiped her hands on a damp rag and looked about with pride tinged with anxiety.

'Not at all, why should I?' he grinned. 'It's a free world so they say. Besides which I'm established — been here a few years and know my way about. For instance what sort of challenge are you going to be hidden away like this? Most punters make for the high street which is why I can charge exorbitant prices. I assume you are going for the lower end of the market?'

Angeline frowned. She didn't like his attitude but chose to say nothing.

'Are you an artist?' he asked picking up one of her sketches off a table which was serving as a counter. 'Going to sell your own work — that's what I heard.'

'I have some paintings of my own to display,' she murmured, carrying on with the unpacking trying her best to ignore his remarks.

'The name's Jeremy by the way as you can see — Jeremy Laporte — it's French.'

Angeline watched him surreptitiously as he examined her work but made no move to offer to shake his hand. 'Angeline Frost,' she said quietly and carried on with her work. 'I'm English.'

'Not bad,' he muttered, but added somewhat haughtily, 'for an amateur. You would have done much better coming straight to me and I'd have put on an exhibition for you. Better in the long run, and it would be cheaper than paying for your own shop.'

Angeline had already noted the surprised look which he hastily covered up. 'Actually I'm not exactly an amateur, I have had it on good authority that my work is of a high standard.'

Browsing round the shop he muttered. 'You mustn't get carried away by friends and family and what they say. They only tell you what they think you want to hear.'

'Oh, but it wasn't. He was an art connoisseur,' she replied tartly, wondering what Russell would think of her description of him.

Jeremy's eyebrows rose marginally. 'Don't forget all the other expenditure — the solicitor, the accountant, etc.'

'I already employ an accountant and a solicitor.'

That did indeed surprise him. Shrugging his shoulders he headed for the door. 'Fancy a drink tonight? Celebrate your new venture?'

She had been going to have an early night but decided that she shouldn't turn down his invitation, he might give her a few tips — unintentionally.

'That would be nice,' she said. 'It's very kind of you to be so accommodating.'

He obviously didn't expect her to be in business long.

'Call for you at eight,' he said

grinning like a Cheshire cat and sauntered off back towards the market square.

Angeline rocked back on her heels thoughtfully. Was this a mistake? Would it have been better to have gone for a more upmarket site? She stared about her remembering how she had been so delighted when she first saw it. It had felt right then and it felt right now. She wasn't going to be intimidated by some brash young man trying to undermine her confidence.

She only had to think of the attractive room above the shop which had such superb views across the roof-tops to the fells beyond. One look at that panoramic spectacle had sold the property to her. She began clearing up the miscellaneous packaging and tidying up the floor space smiling wryly. Russell would certainly approve. It was at his instigation after all.

★ ★ ★

*Angelines* opened on the first Monday in August with a bang — a thunderstorm to be precise. She was very disappointed because it meant the holidaymakers tended to stay close to the shopping mall out of the rain. She couldn't blame them, it's only what she would have done in their place. Very few people even glanced in the window, and by lunch time she could count on one hand the number of browsers even. During the afternoon the weather brightened and gradually the visitors started to venture away from the centre.

She didn't expect hordes of customers queuing up to buy her work, but she did hope some interest would be shown in it. Rather than sit twiddling her thumbs she started on a pencil drawing of the alleyway and the shops nearby. It helped pass the time and may interest local shopkeepers. They had been extremely helpful — loaning her time and tools. She hadn't even a hammer or a sweeping brush to begin with. They were also fulsome with their advice which tended to get a bit monotonous after a while.

She didn't expect to see Jeremy, their meeting the other evening hadn't been a howling success. As she suspected he had only wanted to pump her to find out what her intentions were. She thought he was perhaps more worried than he was letting on, and the high cost of maintaining a presence on the high street was excessive. Once he learned that she hadn't much stock and wasn't inclined to sell bric-a-brac as a filler he soon lost interest and started telling her about his own success story.

★ ★ ★

A week later Angeline was shutting shop when Jeremy arrived outside.

'Just thought I'd pop by to see how you are doing.'

She smiled. 'Fine thank you. It's been a good week. Better than I ever expected.'

111

That threw him for a moment, but then he grinned good naturedly. 'I know — you always have to put a good face on it. The weather hasn't been too kind has it?'

'Not ideal but it kept the tourists in town instead of out on the fells so it helped that way.'

Jeremy had been wandering round clearly unimpressed, but suddenly spied a painting which excited him greatly. He peered at it as if he couldn't believe his eyes. 'Where did you acquire it?' he demanded without tearing his gaze from the canvas.

Angeline, who had been preoccupied sorting out some brushes, looked across to see what he was pointing at with mounting curiosity. She didn't think she would have anything which he would deign to accept as worthwhile — certainly not one of her own work. It turned out to be one of her mother's which she had brought with her from Scarcliff. It was of Mossdale — a wintry scene and extremely eye-catching. Angeline herself liked it enormously, but for a moment wondered if perhaps she had over-priced it or something.

'It's very nice isn't it? It was part of a private collection.'

'You mean you have others?' he asked in a strangled voice.

She frowned and stopped what she was doing. She went over to join him, intrigued by his interest. 'A few, why?'

He bent to examine the signature more closely as if he couldn't believe his eyes. 'Are you sure it's genuine?' he murmured getting out a pocket magnifying glass and examining it minutely.

She almost laughed at his amazement. 'Oh, yes. No doubt about it. Why the interest?'

He turned to her, his face serious — almost angry. 'Because that is one of my mother's early works. I'd like to know how you came by it.'

Angeline was stunned. She took a step back and gulped nervously.

'But . . . but . . . are you sure?'

'Course I'm sure,' he snarled. 'Where did you get?'

Angeline objected to his forthright interrogation. He had no right to speak to her in such a manner. 'I've told you, it was a private transaction,' she said quietly. She turned towards the door intimating that she wanted him to leave. 'Now if that is all, I would like to close the shop. It's been a long day and it is well past closing time.'

He stood his ground looking as if he'd like to shake the truth out of her. 'Let me see what else you have of Jeannie Laporte,' he growled.

Angeline sighed and rolled her eyes. 'I didn't know her name was Laporte, it's only signed Jeannie L.' She showed him the other paintings which she had ready to display, but refrained from mentioning others which she hadn't yet sent for. She had been going to ask Marcus to pack them up and send them on, but then had second thoughts and decided to make the trip back to

Scarcliff herself. Marcus had already suggested taking her out to celebrate her birthday which would be a suitable opportunity to collect the rest of the canvases.

Jeremy's face grew more and more bleak, but Angeline was too taken up with the shock he'd given her to notice. Finally with a grunt of annoyance he marched out leaving Angeline staring after him totally bewildered. How was it possible they had the same mother? She should have asked him for more details. Who was his father for instance and was his mother still alive? There must be a mistake somewhere.

That evening she thought and thought but was no nearer a solution, and there was no one else she could ask except Jeremy. Marcus was hardly likely to have known her mother, and he didn't know the first thing about paintings and artists.

The next morning Angeline decided to delay opening the shop until she'd had time to call on Jeremy. First thing in the morning wasn't a particularly busy time so she hoped she would find him alone at the gallery, which was fortunately the case.

'Hello,' he greeted her none too enthusiastically.

'Jeremy,' she said quietly. 'Could I . . . I wonder if . . . What you said yesterday . . . about Jeannie Laporte being your mother. Is she still alive?'

'Of course. Blind but alive.'

'Blind?'

'Almost. That's what's so annoying. Those pictures you have are some of the last ones she did before her eyesight began to fail.'

Angeline's face expressed the horror of what he said. Licking her dry lips she asked. 'Where . . . where does she live?'

'In France of course with my father. She's never set foot in England for years. You know if you're going to make a success in business it's as well to know something about the artists.'

He sounded scornful. She knew he

was right too. She had jumped in to the new venture too quickly without preparing the ground. She had been so pleased with herself for filling her shop with pictures — many of which were from local amateurs. It had been a brain-wave asking the local art club if they wished to display some of their work. Now she was beginning to wish she had never left Scarcliff.

Possible customers started arriving so she left, walking back to her own premises deep in thought, wondering how her mother and Jeremy's could be one and the same. He was older than her — by several years she guessed. She wished she'd felt able to ask him more about his family. He said his mother was still alive, and yet her own father believed Jeannie had died. Who was telling the truth?

It troubled her for days but she couldn't see any way of resolving the problem until one day Jeremy arrived as she was once again about to shut shop.

'Busy?' he asked, casually looking round at the goods on display. She sensed he was looking for any more paintings by Jeannie L.

She shrugged. 'It's early days yet. Rome wasn't built in a day, or so they say.'

After ascertaining that he'd seen all he was interested in he went to stand by the front window, hands in pockets, staring at one of her mother's painting. 'I have a favour to ask,' not even looking in her direction. He jangled keys in his pockets somewhat irritably.

She was surprised by his words; tilting her head to one side she waited for him to continue.

He eventually turned towards her and smiled. 'How do you fancy a spot of dinner?'

She shook her head. 'I've a cold chicken salad awaiting me upstairs and I can't wait to put my feet up.'

'I don't suppose there's enough for two is there?' he asked with a shrug of the shoulders. 'I have something to discuss with you which is a shade awkward.'

He did look somehow embarrassed she thought.

'I dare say I can stretch it to make sufficient for two if you're not too hungry.'

She led the way up to her flat and showed him into the sitting room.

He whistled when he saw the view. 'Very nice. Come to think of it this isn't a bad little set up you have here.'

'I like it,' she murmured, pleased by his response. 'Make yourself at home while I rustle us up some food.'

She organised the salad, added some cooked ham to go with the chicken, and opened up a tin of fruit to eat with some ice cream. When she returned to the lounge a short while later Jeremy was idly watching the television, but he jumped up immediately and offered to help her lay the table.

'What was it you wanted to see me about?' she asked once they were seated at the small table in front of the window. 'Do help yourself to the salad.' She offered him a bread roll.

He was obviously having great difficulty in coming out with what was on his mind. Finally he looked her full in the face. 'How do you fancy a trip to Paris?'

'Paris?' she gasped, choking on a crumb that had lodged in her throat.

'Not with me,' he hastened to add. 'My . . . my mother wishes to meet with you. She asked me to ask you.'

Angeline was stunned. 'I don't . . . Why?' she gasped eventually, floundering at the unexpected request.

'I rang my mother and told her about the paintings, and she is intrigued as I am to know where you obtained them. Like I told you she doesn't travel much these days, but she offered to meet you in Paris, and to pay for your air fare.'

Angeline was overwhelmed by the prospect of meeting the women who may well turn out to be her own mother. She wanted to accept straight-away, but she was also nervous at the prospect, wondering if she ought to even try to uncover the past. She had become used to the idea that she was without close relatives. Besides if this Jeannie L was her mother she would have a great deal of explaining to do. She had supposedly feigned her own death after dumping her child on her own sister. Why?

'What about my business?' Angeline said to give herself some breathing space. 'I can't . . . '

Jeremy helped himself to the salad and mayonnaise. 'Please, Angie. It would mean so much to her. She's blind, or almost blind, and has been for many years. It would be good for you too, to learn something about the artist. It's not often one gets the opportunity you know, you ought to grasp it with both hands. Most artists are recluses. If you are going to display her work it will vastly improve the saleability if you can speak from experience about having met her.'

There was no answer to that, but he didn't know what he was asking her to do.

'Where would I fly from? I've never been to Paris. How would I find . . . '

'I'll take care of everything,' he said cutting her short, taking her words as acceptance. 'Mother will be pleased. She gets so few visitors and suggested Friday of next week. That is when she will be in Paris for the weekend.'

'But I can't . . . ' Angeline stuttered staring at her plate with unseeing eyes. She needed time to get used to the idea.

Jeremy, unaware of her mounting turmoil blithely told her what arrangements he would put in place making it sound like a holiday. 'Of course you can. I'll take you to the airport myself. You will be met off the plane and driven to our flat in the centre of Paris where mother will be waiting. It couldn't be easier. I wish I could come with you, but unfortunately that is not possible. I will also arrange for someone to look after your shop while you are a way. Mother was most insistent that you were not to lose out monetarily.'

He smiled happily now that he had got his own way. 'You'll love Paris. You should pay a visit to the left bank while you are there. You might even buy some works of art since you seem to have the knack of spotting a bargain.'

# 5

The limousine swept along the wide roads choked with rush hour traffic. Angeline was wishing with every mile that she was safely back in Scarcliff, and that she had taken Marcus's advice and never left. What was she doing speeding through a foreign city heading for who knows what? She ought at least to have told Marcus what she was doing. Someone ought to know where she was apart from Jeremy.

Taking a deep breath she took herself to task. Hadn't she wanted to be an intrepid adventurer not so long ago? What about all those fancy ideas about travelling the world — back packing, etc.? She wouldn't have got far if she couldn't even face a trip to Paris — all arranged too, so that she only had to pack an overnight case.

She settled back in her seat trying

to compose herself, wondering if what she was wearing was suitable for such an auspicious occasion, and then realised that she was being silly. Her mother — the woman she was to meet was nearly blind so what did it matter in the slightest what she wore. Fingering the locket which she believed had been her mother's, she watched with fascination as the driver manoeuvred his way through the chaotic traffic.

At long last the car pulled into a side street away from the hurly burly and drew into the forecourt of a block of flats. The chauffeur got out and helped Angeline to alight before taking her solitary bag from the boot.

'This way,' he said in a gruff foreign accent, and led her through the palatial front door, across an austere marble tiled floor to the lift.

Angeline would like to have practised her limited French on him, to thank him for collecting her at the airport and transporting her safely, but his manner was brusque, so she nodded her thanks with a smile.

'Third floor,' he told her, and left her with the luggage to await the lift.

Left to her own devices Angeline did contemplate walking up the stairs, not over enamoured by the appearance of the ancient contraption, but then decided against it. She wouldn't want to arrive breathless and harassed. The meeting was going to be nerve racking enough without making matters worse. She wished now that she hadn't agreed to stay the night. It would have been feasible to make the trip in a day.

The lift arrived. She was the only person to get aboard and it sped upwards, jerkily pausing at each floor. Angeline's heart was in her mouth when the doors opened, in truth not sure what to expect. A woman, she took to be a maid dressed all in black, not even relieved by a white collar greeted her.

'Mademoiselle Frost?' the maid enquired, her face bland of any emotion.

'Yes . . . Oui,' said Angeline, mentally kicking herself as the stern looking woman took care of her case and directed her into the lounge. The room was deserted. It was a magnificent room sparingly furnished with deep pile carpet, plush sofas and antique furniture. A mirror over the fireplace reflected the dazzling chandelier making the room appear large and airy.

'Madame will be with you shortly. I'll put your case in your room. Please make yourself comfortable.' The maid left.

As instructed Angeline tried to make herself at home. Home she thought — no this wasn't a home. This was a beautifully maintained flat, not a home. There were no photographs on the sideboard, no flowers either, everything was too immaculate.

She wandered over to the window — a large floor length window which opened on to a balcony. She peered down to the street far below and saw the swarming traffic, vaguely hearing noisy horns as irritated drivers gesticulated with each other. It looked so — foreign. The inescapable Eiffel Tower dominated the skyline to her right, but all she was conscious of was the tightness in her chest. Clenching and unclenching her fingers trying to relieve the tension she shivered for no apparent reason. She wasn't cold — far from it she felt flushed. The room was pleasantly warm.

'I hope you had a good flight.'

The soft gentle voice speaking perfect English made her spin round in alarm. She hadn't heard the woman enter and it was strange to hear her speak without the accent which had been so much in evidence since she had set out that morning.

'Yes . . . oui merci,' Angeline said. For a moment her feet seemed entrenched in the sumptuous pile carpet and wouldn't move. Her mouth was dry and for some reason she felt afraid. Recovering quickly, remembering her hostess's blindness, she crossed the room towards the woman.

'Please take a seat. I'm so glad you came.' It was a courteous, well modulated voice with only a hint of an accent.

The woman was by now sitting in a chair by the fireside. Angeline took a seat on the brocade sofa opposite, trying not to appear too curious as she observed her, seeking some sort of recognition. A few moments went by when neither spoke. The woman was the first to break the silence.

'You must be wondering why I asked for this meeting. I hope Jeremy didn't bully you too much, my dear. As he no doubt informed you I am almost blind so I don't travel much these days. I can see sufficiently well to get around the apartment unaided, so prefer to remain on familiar territory. I like to retain what little independence I can.'

She was a slim, graceful woman with salt and pepper coloured hair clipped back from her face, and she wore dark glasses which hid her eyes. Her face was pale and thin but welcoming and friendly. Angeline imagined that she had once been beautiful and even now had a natural charm — an aristocratic elegance. She sat erect with her hands in her lap.

'I understand,' Angeline said quietly twisting a handkerchief into knots. She felt certain that she was about to unravel the mystery of her birth. There was a definite resemblance to the figure in the photographs in the trunk. For an instant she could see a resemblance to her Aunt Sarah too.

'May I . . . Could I ask if you are my mother?'

A sharp intake of breath confirmed her suspicions. 'Who told you that?' the woman demanded, a slight wobble in her voice.

Angeline paused before replying. She hadn't meant to be so outspoken. 'I could say you did,' she said softly, 'because I see you have an identical locket to mine, but in fact I believe it was my father who told me. At least I think he was my father.'

'Was? You mean he's dead? Richard is dead?' Her face paled even more.

'Yes,' Angeline said in little more than a whisper, sorry that she was the bearer of bad news. 'If Richard Frost was my father — he died earlier this year.'

The woman sighed, and seemed to visibly shrink into the cushions. Before she could say anything further the maid brought in a tray of tea which she deposited on a coffee table between them and left. There was also some petit fours and small chocolate fancies.

Angeline wondered if she would be expected to serve the tea, but before she got round to asking, Madame Laporte gathered herself together and proceeded to pour the tea in a strangely well co-ordinated manner.

'Please help yourself,' she said, settling back in her chair again, stroking her forehead anxiously. 'I'm sorry, but this has all been quite a shock. I knew Sarah had died, but . . . I had better explain and then perhaps you can tell me your story. As you have guessed already, I believe I am your mother. The lockets I bought years ago in Japan, and gave one to Sarah as a present. I kept the other as a memento. I don't wear much jewellery these days.

'Jeremy tells me that you have ravishingly gorgeous auburn hair the colour of maple syrup, cinnamon flecked eyes, and that you are elegant, tall, slim and exceedingly beautiful. That's his description and if it is correct, that plus the ownership of my paintings leads me to accept the truth. I don't think there can be two people of that description called Angeline Frost. Quite a coincidence that you two should meet — and in Mossdale of all places.'

Angeline gasped and hurriedly put down her cup and saucer. It was only what she had come to expect, but somehow having it spelt out took her breath away.

'I'm sorry, my dear. That was

thoughtless of me. I shouldn't have been so forthright.' The woman paused again and looked a shade distraught.

'Jeremy exaggerates,' Angeline said. 'I'm not beautiful, my nose is too large and I have lots of freckles.'

'Beauty is in the eye of the beholder don't forget,' her mother said. 'I'm sure if I could see you clearly I too would think you beautiful — you certainly were as a baby. A contented little scrap who clung so tenaciously to life.

'My name as you are now aware is Jeannie Laporte. I married Henri Laporte and we have the one son, Jeremy. What I have to tell you is to be in the utmost confidence, just between the two of us. That is why I chose to have this meeting here where we can be discreet. No one else must ever know. Henri has no knowledge of my indiscretion with your father. Yes, my dear, I did have an affair with my sister's husband — if you can call one night's aberration an affair. I suppose that scandalises you? I hope you will bear with me and hopefully understand and forgive.'

Angeline fingered the locket, speechless. Ever since Jeremy's disclosure she had been confident that Jeannie Laporte was going to turn out to be her mother, but somehow now that it was confirmed she was finding it difficult to credit. She wasn't sure how she expected to feel, but not the calm acceptance of the moment. This woman was her mother — the person who had given birth to her — who had given her away, and yet she felt pleased to meet her. That surprised her. She felt no animosity towards her, only curiosity.

'Henri and I met at art school,' her mother continued. 'We fell in love and travelled extensively, seeing the world and enjoying a gypsy lifestyle. I didn't know at the time that Henri was heir to a wealthy estate. He kept that very quiet. We married when I became pregnant, but continued with our contented freedom, until one day he heard that his father had died. That was when he told me about his well-to-do background, and that he had to return to take over the running of the family estate.

'I suddenly realised that I didn't know him at all. Ten years we had lived together and yet he was a stranger. As he read the letter his manner altered before my very eyes — he became the autocrat he'd been born to be. We packed our bags and returned to France, but naturally I was bewildered by the whole scene. I couldn't cope with what it entailed. I wasn't used to such grandiose surroundings, servants, possessions, fancy clothes and influential people one had to meet. I know I should have been thrilled to bits — or so I was told, but instead I felt miserable. Sarah would have been in her element but not me.

'Anyway, I'd received word from my sister that she was married — rather late in life, and she was unwell, so I made it an excuse to pay her a visit. I hadn't seen her for ages. We had never been close because of the age gap, but Henri thought it a good idea for me to go. In fact he positively urged me to do so. He was having enough trouble himself settling down to what was expected of him after our footloose existence. At the time we were both irritable with each other trying to come to terms with the changing lifestyle.

'I left Jeremy with Henri — he was six years old and needed to start proper schooling. That was one of the things we argued about. I wanted Jeremy to go to the local village school, but Henri insisted he attend a boarding school — the one he'd attended apparently. I couldn't fight both him and his mother, so I gave in and went to Scarcliff alone — for a holiday initially.

'Sarah had been married quite a while and was miserable because she hadn't become pregnant and blamed her husband. In the circumstances when I arrived I thought it best not to reveal that I was married and had a child. Sarah assumed I was still unattached so I didn't acquaint her with my marital status. After the rows Henri and I had been having I was wondering for how much long I would be married anyway.

'Richard I thought was charming — a real gentleman. He made me very welcome when I arrived with my goods and chattels, and provided space in the room over the garage for me to continue painting. Painting was my life, that was the problem. Henri found it easier to step into the new role while I couldn't. My whole way of life had been turned up-side-down.

'I loved being back in Scarcliff and I soon settled to my painting, losing all track of time. Richard was often sent to fetch me for meals otherwise I would forget to eat, I was so wrapped up in my work. He, bless him used to fuss over me. He worried about my health and some times we spent hours chatting — mainly about music.

'He was beginning to have some difficulty playing the piano due to the onset of arthritis and needed tea and sympathy occasionally. Sarah was inclined to bully him, but he was so sensitive and her approach made him insecure. But Richard and I got on really well together. The three of us used to drive up the coast and stop off at quaint little tea rooms for hot toasted teacakes and cream sponges I remember.

'I thought I was helping — helping both of them — doing simple things like walking along the beach barefoot, paddling in the sea after dark and so on. Sarah was always so stiff and starchy and I wanted to lighten things up. She was so up tight, which wasn't doing her chances of conceiving any good — not at her age.

'I returned to France for Christmas and New Year, but it wasn't a success. Henri and I argued — mainly about his mother. She didn't like me and made my life impossible, criticising everything I did, especially the way I dressed and the way I was bringing up her grandson. Poor Jeremy hated the school he'd been banished to, so it was a miserable time for all concerned.

I returned to Scarcliff trying to come to a decision about what I wanted to do with my life. I still loved Henri in a fashion, but he'd changed, he'd become too dominated by his mother who was a pretty cantankerous individual.

'One evening — it was Richard's birthday. Sarah arranged a small cocktail party in his honour. She invited a few local dignitaries and friends round, and put on quite a spread. It was quite a grand affair, but unfortunately the work involved in preparing it was too much for her. She developed one of those migraine headaches she was prone to enjoying. By ten o'clock she had to retire to her room. The party gradually dispersed and I was left alone with Richard. By then we'd had a few drinks and Richard suggested a walk round the garden before turning in.

'It was such a beautiful night. The full moon cast a silver pathway across the water, and the air was crystal clear with a hint of frost. It was a night made for lovers and I'm afraid we succumbed. Our stroll took us to the studio, and you can guess the rest. It was my fault. I accept the blame for what happened. We were two poor souls comforting each. Richard never looked at another woman, he worshipped Sarah.' She shook her head sadly. 'Afterwards he felt so guilty. We both did, but I'm the one to blame, not Richard.'

Angeline shook her head. 'Just before he died dad informed me that he was my real father. He told me about you and said he was the one at fault. After mum died he became confused. Until then I believed I had been adopted by my aunt and uncle, and that you — my mother had died soon after I was born.'

Jeannie Laporte pursed her lips. 'I knew if Richard even half suspected you were his daughter he would want to tell Sarah everything and offer to take care of me, but I still thought I loved Henri. It was difficult accepting the way Henri wanted me to live. It was a terrible predicament I found myself in.

'Besides I couldn't break up their marriage — my own sister and brother-in-law. It was a moment of sheer folly, which wouldn't have happened if Sarah hadn't retired early with migraine. Richard really did love her. He thought the world of her. He kept telling me what a wonderful wife she was.' She stirred her tea thoughtfully. 'You were such a beautiful baby, Angeline, but delicate. At one stage I feared for your life, and knew that I had to do something positive for all our sakes.'

'How did you explain about . . . ?'

'I lied, I'm afraid. I told Sarah that I'd had an affair with a married man but couldn't reveal his name. It was the truth, for at the time I wasn't sure who was your father. You see I didn't realise I was pregnant for a long time. I felt fine, I wasn't sick and I didn't put on weight. It was more than four months before I found out, and that was only because Sarah insisted I saw a doctor friend of theirs. I had a summer cold that lingered too long in her view.

'She was furious when she learned of my condition, and we had a dreadful row. She accused me of bringing shame to the family name. I'm not sure if she ever suspected Richard — she never said so openly. She liked to bury her head in the sand at times did Sarah. If it wasn't discussed openly then she could overlook anything, especially bad things and pretend they never happened.'

'So . . . who is my father?' Angeline asked appalled.

'I wasn't sure. How could I be? After the upset with Sarah I decided to go to Mossdale where I had previously spent some time painting after I left college. I wanted time to pluck up the courage to tell Henri about being pregnant, hoping he would be charitable. He has a temper at times has Henri and I didn't know how he would take the

142

news. It was quite possible that he would throw me out, bag and baggage, and I would never see my son again.

'If he thought he wasn't the father this time he would have made my life hell. He hinted sometimes when we were arguing that the marriage service we went through wasn't legitimate. I think he only said it to make me anxious because I knew he would never let go of his son. Jeremy is his heir and would one day have control of the estate. A man in his position would always have the law on his side, so there was nothing I could do, but I couldn't bear never to see Jeremy again. So I stayed on in Mossdale until after you were born hoping that something — some small detail would convince me who was the father. I felt there had to be a way of knowing.'

'Was there?' Angeline asked, dreading the answer.

Her mother gave a weak smile. 'As it happened I found I didn't want to know. During the latter part of my pregnancy my eyesight started to deteriorate — not too badly to begin with, but it was sufficient to make me stop and think seriously about my circumstances. If I couldn't paint what was I to do? How would I live?

'I finally accepted that I ought to have tried harder to fit in with Henri's new way of life and that I was being selfish staying away for so long. Jeremy needed me to be strong for both our sakes. That was when I made my decision. I would give Sarah the one thing she wanted — a child to nurture. If it was Richard's child then it would be going to the right home anyway, and if it was Henri's — well . . . He didn't deserve you.

'The cross I had to bear was that I knew I had to find a way out of the mess I had made of my life, and that in doing so I would never see you again. I was determined to go through with my plan even after you were born and I held you in my arms. I suppose you will think I was heartless and cruel — cold bloodedly deciding to give my baby away.

'I can't expect you to understand or condone what I did, but I hope you will accept that I did it with a heavy heart, and with the true belief that it was in your best interest.

'I rang Sarah. At first she was angry and on her high horse, but when I explained that I was ill she immediately volunteered to look after us both. Underneath her cool reserve there beat a heart of gold. I spun them a yarn about some specialist that I wanted to visit who might be able to help, and left you in their care knowing that you would be cherished as if you were their very own.

'Then I rang Henri and told him that I had finished painting for good, that I wanted to return and be his wife again. He appeared delighted although didn't exactly welcome me back with open arms. But when he heard about my eye problem he was extremely sympathetic. He insisted I visit anyone who could possibly help, but sadly my eyesight got progressively worse.

'For a while though things were good between us. Henri was patient as I tried to slip into the role I had agreed to play, and even his mother relaxed her dislike of me sufficiently to offer her assistance. I tried very hard as a way of expunging my guilt, and I became the competent chatelaine Henri desired. He had a position in the community which had to be upheld, and of course there was also our son on whom I doted.'

She took a sip of tea before continuing.

'There was no way I could have managed to keep you all alone, steadily going blind. I know it must sound horribly cold and calculating, but I truly believed, and still believe what I did was for the best. There was no other conceivable solution — I had to die as far as Sarah and Richard were concerned, and giving you to them to bring up was the obvious solution.'

Angeline was enthralled. It was like a

fairy story. 'However did you manage to arrange to convince them of your death? Surely they would want to attend the funeral?'

Jeannie gave a watery smile. 'It wasn't too difficult. I wrote telling them that I was to have an operation and that they were not to worry. I sounded optimistic, that the prognosis was good and that I would soon be returning to Scarcliff. Then I sent them notification of my demise — by proxy of course — too late to attend a funeral. They thought I never recovered consciousness after the operation. And of course they were having to cope with bringing up a baby, which was no mean feat at their age don't forget. I have spent the rest of my life trying to make up to my husband for my infidelity. It would destroy Henri if he ever learns the truth.'

'So he knows nothing about me at all?'

'No and he must never find out. I've hurt enough people in my life. I hope that you feel the same? I know it's asking a lot of you, but there's nothing to be gained by revealing the truth now is there?'

Angeline nodded and then realised her error and agreed unequivocally. 'I'm glad to know what really happened, but as you say it makes little difference now. I've become used to the idea of being alone in the world.' It wasn't strictly accurate, but she felt obliged to pacify her mother in view of what she had been told. Better to remain friends she thought, and she did feel some affection for her. She could understand her motives.

'I had to see you,' her mother said, 'to explain, mainly because Jeremy has become a great fan of yours. I could see all sorts of complications looming and wanted to nip it in the bud.'

'There is nothing between us,' Angeline said with a rueful smile. 'I started up a business in Mossdale, but Jeremy is scornful of my puny attempt to compete.'

'That's not what he told me. He was

impressed with your work. He wished he could display it in his gallery. I gather you have talent.'

Once they got talking it was amazing how the time flew by, and Angeline's natural reserve was soon overcome. Her mother was an interesting and at times amusing companion covering a wide range of topics.

# 6

'Having spoken to your mother I have decided to take her advice and spend more time painting. Jeannie suggested that perhaps we could go into partnership. What do you think?' Angeline crossed her fingers behind her back. She was grossly exaggerating what Jeannie had said and hoped that Jeremy didn't consult his mother about business matters.

'Not a bad idea I suppose,' Jeremy replied thoughtfully. 'You have a certain flair for expressing yourself on canvas that appeals to the touristy element, and your good looks are a definite asset. You could probably charm the waverers by flashing them one of those artless smiles of yours and they would buy anything.'

Angeline bit her lip refusing to be drawn by his insulting tone.

'I would need a lot more paintings than what you have here though. And you did intimate that you had more of my mother's work.' Jeremy's eyes gleamed at the prospect.

'Yes,' she said cautiously. 'I have access to another half a dozen or so canvases.'

'OK then, it's a deal. I'll have a lawyer arrange the paperwork.'

Angeline was thrilled that she had actually pulled it off. She hadn't believed she could remain so calm negotiating with Jeremy. She could now stay in her flat which she loved, and paint which she also loved, and best of all the Mossdale Arts club could keep their outlet open. They would have to man it themselves in future, but it was all quite feasible. She was also thankful that he hadn't pressed her as to where she obtained her mother's paintings.

She was so pleased with herself that she rang Marcus to tell him that she was returning to Scarcliff the following weekend. She wanted to discuss the deal with him to make sure she hadn't overlooked something significant. To begin with Jeremy had been hesitant about showing her the financial status of the Laporte Gallery, but the thought of getting his hands on more of his mother's paintings soon overcame his reluctance.

As she had suspected things were not quite so rosy as he tried to make out, but she still thought it would be a sound business deal. It would give her the opportunity to do what she was best at and still have some income from the gallery. It wouldn't make her a millionaire but it was a step in the right direction — that is if Marcus didn't find anything untoward. He was much better at reading balance sheets and such like. She even thought he would welcome the opportunity to come to her aid. Whenever she spoke to him he seemed eager to help and keen to see her.

She was looking forward to seeing him again. It had been months since they met — since she'd made the break from Scarcliff. She missed him. She had a photograph of him taken some time ago in the back garden of the Viking Lodge, and it now resided on her bedside table. Marcus looked relaxed and virile in open necked shirt and slacks, laughing at the antics of a squirrel running along the back wall. That was how she liked to remember him. The easy going companion of her childhood, but she wished they could have progressed into a more intimate relationship now that she was no longer a child.

The time apart had made her realise how much she loved him, not only as a friend but more than that. The other men she came into contact with didn't measure up to how she felt about him. He had a presence all of his own — dictatorial one minute, but concerned and compassionate the next. Lucky Fiona she thought miserably. What wouldn't she give to be in her shoes and see Marcus every day. She wondered why they hadn't married before now, they had been together for many years. Perhaps — just perhaps they weren't emotionally involved she thought wistfully.

She dialled the number with a smile on her face. She wondered if the house was all right and if Terry was still maintaining the gardens satisfactorily. Marcus could be quite a tyrant in business matters — not the easy going employer her father had been. He hadn't been too keen on Terry remaining at the flat, but Angeline felt it best to leave things as they were for the time being. Terry could keep an eye on the property and discourage prowlers, and also, she hated to admit it, but she still felt a certain fondness for him. She wouldn't go so far as to say she was passionately in love with him, but a lingering sort of longing.

Fiona answered wiping away her happiness, her crisp business-like voice enunciating clearly that she was through to Stone Associates.

'Marcus will be delighted to see you I'm sure,' Fiona said, her tone lacking enthusiasm. 'I believe we were going away for the day on Saturday, but I'm sure Marcus will spare some time for you, perhaps on Sunday. He has a big case on at the moment so is extremely busy, but I'll let him know you called.'

Angeline's spirits plummeted. 'Oh, I may delay it for another week then. I'll speak to Marcus when he's free to see when it's convenient. Please tell him I have something I wish to discuss with him. Something I need his advice about.'

Angeline was miserable for no apparent reason. She knew Marcus had been seeing Fiona for several years now, so it shouldn't surprise her to hear that they intended spending some time together. Somehow it depressed her though. She always thought she only had to pick up the phone and Marcus would be there. He was her lifeline — so stable and predictable. She didn't like to think about him possibly getting married — and to Fiona. Oh no, she wouldn't like that at all. She was too old for Marcus. He would be thirty next birthday and Fiona must be nearer forty she surmised.

'You look sad,' Jeremy said arriving as she put the phone down. 'What has caused the frown on your pretty face?'

Angeline brightened up and grimaced. 'You know that's not true. I've not got a pretty face. My nose is too big for a start and I'm covered in freckles.'

'I never even noticed,' Jeremy said taking hold of her face and positioning it so that he could examine it carefully. 'You have such interesting features that to me you are beautiful. You could have been a model. You remind me of someone but I can't put my finger on who.'

Angeline was pleased by his attempt to pacify her even though she knew it to be untrue, but she didn't wish him to ponder on her any resemblance to his mother. She sighed. 'I was going to go back to Scarcliff this weekend but I find that the person I want to see isn't available.'

'Well then perhaps you will accept my invitation.'

'What invitation?' she laughed. 'I don't remember you asking me to go anywhere.'

'I desire the pleasure of your company,' he said in all seriousness. 'It is my birthday on Sunday and I have no wish to celebrate alone. Perhaps we could spend the day on the lake. My friend has a small motor boat I could borrow.'

He was quite persuasive and in the end she agreed. She couldn't see any harm in spending a day in his company since they were going to be business partners. He was after all cheerful and sophisticated, and he probably had numerous girl friends. She ought to think herself lucky to be asked. She didn't think his mother would be pleased if she heard, but that was hardly likely.

The weather was cloudy but warm on Sunday as Jeremy steered the craft away from the landing place and Angeline sat on a padded seat at the side of the boat.

'You never told me much about your trip to Paris,' Jeremy observed neatly clearing the last of the moorings before heading for some small islands at the far side of the lake. 'Did you enjoy yourself?'

'Yes, I did,' Angeline admitted. 'Your mother was charming. It is such a shame she had to give up painting. I don't know what I would do if that happened to me.'

Jeremy concentrated on setting a course across the lake. 'She's extremely supportive. My father keeps her busy at the chateau making certain she is never bored. She has come to live with her disability very well. I've never known her moan about how badly done to she is. She's fond of music, and even mastered Braille so that she could read. She hates relying on others. She used to be quite a good guitar player and has made tapes of some of her favourites. She won't sell them though. She gives them away, mainly to charities so they can make money.'

'You admire her tremendously don't you?'

'Of course. She's my mother, but she'll always be someone I can look up to with pride for her artistic achievement if nothing else. It's a pity I didn't inherit her artistic talent.'

'Where are we going?' Angeline asked wishing to change the subject. They were getting into dangerous territory.

'I thought we'd have a picnic on yonder island. I hope you brought your sketch pad. It's an artist's paradise or so I've heard.'

She laughed. 'Everywhere is an artist's paradise in this locality. How come you set up in Mossdale? It's a long way from your home town.'

He stood casually holding the wheel looking relaxed and confident — almost arrogant; no aristocratic like his father she decided thoughtfully.

'It was a pure fluke, but a lucky one for me. I had finished my course at business school and was trying to decide what I could do with my life, when out of the blue a friend of my mother died and left her the gallery. He couldn't have heard about her sight problem, so of course, since mother couldn't do anything about the business she gave it to me. It wasn't in any great shakes when I first arrived mind you. The people before me had taken to selling all sorts of grotty souvenirs, but I could see the potential. It's been an uphill struggle ever since, getting it into a profitable condition, especially as I am not an artist like my mother.'

'Didn't you know anything about paintings then?'

'Not as much as I should have, but I didn't let that stop me. I knew what I liked, and of course I talked to mother about the stock that was here when I took over. To begin with I made lots of mistakes, but I soon learned what the customers wanted. They aren't usually looking for Van Gogh's or Picasso's here in Lakeland, but charming local scenes — the chocolate box variety I call them.'

'So you don't miss France?'

'No I don't. I don't feel particularly French, I never have. I feel more English and at home here. I suppose I must take after mother. I believe she used to come here often when she was a child so maybe I inherited the penchant for the area from her. Her parents apparently enjoyed fell walking and thought the fresh air good for her. She was inclined to be delicate as a child I understand.'

'The mountain air must have done her good then. She told me about her exploits, travelling the world with your father, living off whatever they could earn. She had such an interesting existence, but made light of the hardship which they must have endured at times. I wish I had the nerve to do such a thing.'

'I can't somehow see you packing your bags and living like a gypsy,' he chuckled.

'Why not?' she demanded, trailing her hand in the water.

'Because, sweetheart, you are classy and obviously used to a privileged life like me. Ugh, the thought of all those creepy crawlies, snakes and flies and other obnoxious creatures — no they are not for me thank you very much.'

Angeline who had become irritated with a wasp that was intent on landing on her face swiped at it viciously, nearly falling overboard at the same time.

'See what I mean?' he laughed not making any attempt to rescue her. He switched off the engine, slowly manoeuvring the craft to a simple plank that served as a landing place.

The silence was quite awe-inspiring. For a moment Angeline sat absorbing the peaceful scene, thinking about her mother and how sad it was that she could never see it again. It was tragic. It would be for anyone, but doubly so for anyone who itched to paint like she did. The more she thought about Jeannie the more she realised how strong willed she must have been and she admired her for it. She was obviously a complex personality and so different from her sister.

Jeremy disappeared into the small cabin enclosure to collect the picnic basket and a rug. In the mean time Angeline stepped ashore and wandered along the water's edge deep in thought.

'This is idyllic,' Jeremy said happily spreading the rug down in the shade of the one and only tree. It was little more than an overgrown shrub but it did provide some shade. The sun had come out and it was beginning to get quite hot.

Angeline joined him slipping off her cardigan and sitting primly facing the water. 'I gather you've been here before. Is this where you bring all your girl friends?' she remarked jokingly.

'Of course. Here I have them at my mercy — unless they are exceptionally good swimmers,' he leered dangling the boat keys from his index finger and then stowed them away in his pocket.

Angeline pulled a face but wondered for a moment what would happen if he turned awkward. She couldn't swim back to the landing stage, she wasn't that good a swimmer, and there was no-one else around who could come to her rescue. She began to feel a shade apprehensive.

'I don't know about you but I'm famished,' he said delving into the basket. A bottle of wine was produced first, quickly followed by several packages. 'I got the shop on the corner to pack it for me. I wonder what goodies there are?'

'If you like the good life why did you leave home?' she asked, keeping a safe distance from him and helping herself to a chicken leg. 'You could have sold the Gallery. Didn't you live on some sort of estate?'

Jeremy poured the wine and handed

her a glass. 'I wanted to prove that I could do something off my own bat. If I'd stayed at home I'd have been at father's beck and call — all very grand but not fulfilling. Here I'm my own master.'

'You were,' she corrected wagging her chicken bone. 'You now have a partner and don't you forget it.'

He grinned unabashed. 'Hardly likely to. Come here, gorgeous.'

He made a half hearted attempt to grab her but she rolled quickly out of reach. She giggled wanting to keep everything purely platonic since there was no way they could become anything more than friends. She wasn't sure if she even liked him. At times she thought he could be good fun, but at other times he came over as pompous and self opinionated. She had great difficulty in seeing him as her half-brother, or even . . . her brother!

'What sort of estate is it?' she asked.

'Oh, the usual. A large rambling house full of antiques and acres of land — mostly vineyards. Some farms rented out to tenant farmers. Some of the farmhouses are now being renovated and sold off when they become vacant. The people in the village think of father as the feudal Lord of the Manor type of thing, but to me it's a lot of nonsense trying to maintain a heap of old relics without the wherewithal to do the job properly. He has to keep selling bits off it to make ends meet.'

'What a shame,' Angeline said thoughtfully. She was lucky that there was sufficient funds available to maintain her home — more than enough apparently. That brought her back to wondering what she was going to do with Viking Lodge. She loved the house. It was the only home she had ever known. However it was far too big to live in alone. Sometime she was going to have to ask Marcus for his advice.

'I didn't bring you out here to discuss my family and its problems,' Jeremy grimaced. 'It's a glorious day so don't let's spoil it by such talk.'

After they had cleared away the debris of the picnic Angeline lay back and closed her eyes, for a moment enjoying the warm sun and the peace. They had the island to themselves. She thought about her mother again, wondering what it would have been like if she had taken her to France to live there. Would Henri have accepted her in his household as a sister for Jeremy, or would he have always been looking for a likeness and finding none?

She came out in goose pimples. She didn't have a favourable opinion of Henri Laporte, although she didn't know why she thought as she did. She was glad in a way that her mother had left her in England. She'd had a satisfactory childhood — if somewhat lonely, but she couldn't say she had been unhappy like she may well have been if she had gone to the Laporte family home.

'Now for my reward for being such a good boy.' Jeremy leaned over and kissed her, breaking into her day dream. It was only a light brotherly kiss — no big deal. Better not to say anything she thought so keeping her eyes closed she pretended to sleep. She was tired and a bit drowsy from the unaccustomed wine.

Jeremy took the hint and lay down beside her yawning. Stretching out, he pulled her gently into the crook of his arm. Smoothing her hair from her face he bent to kiss her again. This time she wasn't prepared for his masterly domineering stance, pinned as she was by his long lean body. All thoughts of repulsing him disappeared as he coaxed and manipulated her until she was putty in his hands.

'You are incredible, Angie. I knew the moment I set eyes on you that we were meant for each other.'

Startled into action she struggled to sit up but he held her firm depositing butterfly kisses in the hollow between her breasts.

'Please,' she said urgently. 'Please,

Jeremy, what are you saying? What are you doing?'

'I'm in love with you, ma cherie. Didn't mother tell you? I want you.'

She shrieked in alarm and managed to roll away from him.

'What's the matter?' he asked in a hurt tone. 'Surely a bit of petting is allowed. We are alone on this deserted island, not a soul within hearing distance. I know it's not the idyllic tropical place of which fantasies are made, but it's the best I can do for the moment.'

'No, it's not that . . . Oh Jeremy you don't understand, I'm not in love with you. I thought we were friends — as well as partners, but . . . '

He became petulant. 'Is there someone else? Not one of those simpering amateurs you have hanging around surely?'

'No,' she whispered. 'I'm in love with a man I've known all my life.'

Jeremy got to his feet and stood over her, his hands dug deep in his pockets. He was clearly shaken by her disclosure. 'So where is he?' he said shrugging his shoulders and turning to stare out across the lake. 'Where is this fantastic individual? How come he leaves you prey to any hot blooded male? I don't believe he exists. You are making it up. What is his name?'

'His name is Marcus,' she said without thinking. She got up and touched his arm as a friendly gesture but he shook it off impatiently. 'I was to have gone to see him this weekend if you remember,' she continued, 'but he was called away, which is why I am here and able to help you celebrate your birthday.'

'What's he like then this mysterious boy friend?' Jeremy snarled turning to face her. He looked exceedingly angry.

'He's tall, dark and extremely handsome,' Angeline replied with a nervous laugh. 'He is a distinguished solicitor in Scarcliff, and I've known him all my life. He's my guardian too.'

'Sounds a bore.'

'He's not,' she remonstrated, although privately thought Marcus too sober at times, but that was Fiona's influence and she could alter that. 'He may not be a flashy dresser, or go in for wild parties, but he's kind, helpful and considerate.'

'Good grief,' he scoffed. 'Just listen to you. Hardly a passionate love affair by all accounts. Sounds like a cold fish and no mistake.'

★ ★ ★

They returned to Mossdale in subdued mood. Angeline said goodbye outside the gallery. 'Thanks for a lovely time.'

He raised his eyebrows. 'You reckon? I thought we would be spending the evening together.'

She shook her head. 'I don't think that would be a good idea. Anyway, I have work to do. I left the shop in a bit of a mess, and I have pictures to frame for those amateurs you so disparage.'

She turned and almost bumped into a man who had just crossed the road. 'Sorry,' she muttered and would have hurried past but he clutched at her arm.

'Hello, Angel. I hardly recognised you. I've not seen you since you had your hair cut. It suits you.'

'Marcus!' She gulped in amazement. 'How . . . how did you know where to come?' She had so far been most careful not to let him have the address or even the name of the town.

'That wasn't too difficult in this age of modern technology,' he grinned giving her a warm friendly hug. 'I found out the telephone number you were dialling from.'

Angeline blushed when she recalled what she had told Jeremy about being in love with him. She hoped he wouldn't say anything to embarrass her.

'Marcus, I'd like you to meet Jeremy Laporte. We've been on the lake to celebrate Jeremy's birthday.'

'Many happy returns,' Marcus said

pleasantly. 'I hope you have been taking good care of Angel, she's not a very good swimmer.'

'Oh I've taken very good care of her,' Jeremy remarked in a surly tone and walked huffily away. Calling out that he would see her first thing the next day.

★ ★ ★

'Why didn't you tell me you were coming?' Angeline said to Marcus as they walked to her flat hand in hand. She was a little surprised by his friendliness but pleased all the same. He didn't look so stiff and starchy in casual clothes, and he'd let his hair grow longer which suited him — made him look younger.

'I thought I'd surprise you.'

'You have certainly done that. But what about Fiona? She said you were planning to go away together this weekend.'

'I think you must have mis-heard.

I never had any intention of going anywhere this weekend.'

Angeline knew that she hadn't misheard but kept her mouth shut.

'Tell me what you would like to do for the rest of the day?' he asked. 'I hope I haven't spoiled your plans.'

She shook her head. 'I feel a bit dishevelled, so why don't I cook us a meal, unless you'd rather go somewhere? I know a pleasant little pub.'

'If you don't mind I think it would be splendid idea if we stayed in and then you can tell me what you have been up to these last few months. I've had a hectic week and could do to relax a while. The traffic was pretty horrendous coming here so I've booked into a hotel overnight, but I'll have to set off back straight after breakfast. I'm due in court tomorrow afternoon. Who's the young man by the way? He didn't seem pleased to see me. Is he a serious contender for your affections?'

'I don't know what you mean,' she

said coyly. 'Jeremy owns the art gallery of which I am now part owner. He's a friend that's all.'

'Sure?'

'Positive. There will never be anything else between us.'

'Good, because I didn't care for his attitude. Don't forget I'll want to interview all prospective candidates. That is part of my privilege as your guardian.'

She smiled thinking he was teasing. 'I don't need a guardian you know, but I'm so pleased to see you. I want your advice now that I'm going into partnership with Jeremy. I hoped you would give the paperwork the once over.'

'My, my, you do keep on surprising me. I didn't think you'd stick this working lark for long. I would have put money on your returning within a month or so.' He hugged her and deposited a light kiss on her forehead. 'I've missed you, you know. More than I expected. Sure you don't want to come back with me? Maybe I could find you something to do in my office?'

'I don't think that would be a good idea,' she said pleased by his affection, 'but thanks all the same. I am enjoying myself here — most of the time. Make yourself at home. I won't be long.'

She left Marcus looking at the paintings while she had a quick shower and changed her clothes. She rooted out a sheath dress — a recent acquisition, pleased that she had something to wear which Marcus hadn't seen before. It suited her she thought. A quick glance in the mirror confirmed the way it showed off her figure — a womanly shape, not a schoolgirl's anymore. Had Marcus noticed?

The sun tan she was acquiring gave her a healthy glow, and she only hoped it didn't peel. She brushed her hair vigorously, and sought out some dangly earrings, wanting to make the most of her new found composure. She had grown up a lot since she left Scarcliff, and she wanted Marcus to realise how mature she had become. It meant a lot to have him see her as a woman, with a woman's feelings. What she had told Jeremy was in part the truth. She did love Marcus, but she didn't know what his thoughts were about her. He had always behaved towards her like he was her older brother.

'I don't know much about art as you know,' Marcus said when she rejoined him, 'but I rather like some of those hanging on the wall downstairs. I wouldn't mind buying one or two. You say they are done by amateurs?'

'Yes. Jeremy doesn't agree, but I think some of them show promise.'

'You look wonderful, Angie. I can't get over the change in you.' He shook his head. 'Incredible!'

She laughed. 'No — it's the same old me. The same old ugly duckling, just grown up a bit.'

'You were never an ugly duckling,' he chuckled, 'but you have certainly grown into a beautiful young woman. Your father would have been mighty proud to see you right now.'

She smiled, delighted by his compliments. 'Thanks. Now how do you fancy a pizza? That's about all I've got in at the moment.' She recalled at the last minute Marcus's disdain for her partiality to Italian food. 'I'm sorry, perhaps it would be best if we went out.'

He surprised her. 'Pizza's fine. Recently I've become quite partial to it. Fending for myself I often send out for a pizza when I can't be bothered to cook anything. Can I give you a hand?'

'No thanks, you sit and look at the view, and when you've had enough of that you can glance through these papers I told you about.' She handed him a copy of the contract and Jeremy's financial report. 'I hope you don't find anything amiss. I know I won't make a fortune judging by past turnover, but I believe it has the makings of a good business. Jeremy has spent a good deal on furnishings to make it more inviting, which has meant a considerable outlay, so the figures don't look too good I know.'

★ ★ ★

Angeline enjoyed the evening very much. Marcus seemed different. They shared a bottle of wine and sat talking — really talking. He treated her as if she was a grown up for the first time in her life. He asked pertinent questions about the business and gently made suggestions, but didn't come over as the bossy big brother like he used to.

It was the middle of the evening by the time they were washing up in the small kitchen, and even that was fun. Marcus insisting on tying on an apron after losing the toss and having to wash rather than dry. Then sitting on the settee in front of the fire he put his arm affectionately round her as she nestled against him while they talked about the past. It was pleasant recalling the happier times they had spent in each other's company, at concerts, anniversaries and other such gatherings.

At one stage she considered telling him about her trip to Paris, but then realised that she would have to explain everything, and she could get into deep water. Marcus, being a lawyer was the soul of discretion, but she had given her word not to tell anyone about Jeannie being her real mother — it had to remain a secret.

'I'm proud of you, Angel,' Marcus said as he reluctantly got up to go. 'You've done exceedingly well, but don't ever forget where I am. You only have to pick up the phone and I'll be here. I promised your father I would, and in this case I have a vested interest.'

He bent to kiss her. She expected a peck on the cheek as usual, but their lips met. His mouth was soft and inviting. She closed her eyes revelling in a kind of euphoria. She liked the sensation that rippled through her. It reminded her a little of Terry, but this time it was more . . . somehow different, but she couldn't put her finger on it.

'May I come again?' he asked, putting his arms round her waist hugging her to him.

'Of course,' she replied brightly, wishing for more of the same. 'I'd love to see more of you.'

'Would you really, Angie? So you do miss me a little?'

He didn't give her time to answer, but sought her lips again, gently persuading her to respond. His encouragement was all she needed. Sliding her hands round his neck she responded immediately, enjoying his solidity and expertise. Marcus was so, so wonderful. Why hadn't she noticed how handsome he was before now? She liked the familiar scent of cedarwood aftershave. It was his favourite and she had always bought him some for Christmas.

His hands were firm and strong, yet disciplined as they pulled her hard against his lean masculine frame. This was a new exciting Marcus. Someone she felt comfortable with, yet his kisses were stirring emotions within her which electrified her. She recalled Russell's words of advice. Would he approve of Marcus she wondered? She knew the answer to that would be a resounding yes. Marcus was every girl's dream. She snuggled harder against him wanting to show how much she really cared and missed him.

Rifling a hand through her hair he massaged her neck and gently stroked her cheek. Then with one last kiss he set them apart, looked round for his jacket. 'I'd better be going,' he said in a husky uneven voice.

Angeline remained where she was unable to move. It was going to be a long week. She smiled as he stumbled against a chair. It was most unlike Marcus to be clumsy.

★ ★ ★

As she prepared for bed Angeline reviewed her day. The trip with Jeremy had been a mistake. She wondered if he had agreed to the partnership because he thought she was in love with him, in which case the deal wouldn't be significant. She wouldn't have to spend much time with him in future without others being present she realised. That brought her again to Marcus. He was never far from her thoughts. It was comforting to think that he was only just up the road, and she smiled when she recalled that he said he would be back the following weekend. He'd sounded eager to return!

# 7

The past few weeks had been utterly fantastic. Angeline was pleased to find her relationship with Jeremy was reasonably amicable. He'd soon found himself another female companion she noticed wryly. Marcus began spending most weekends in Mossdale, and together they rambled and explored the area. Angeline couldn't remember ever being happier and had to pinch herself often to see that she wasn't dreaming.

During the week her time was spent painting, or manning the Gallery when Jeremy wanted time off, but Sunday was her free day to spend solely with Marcus. She had put her foot down firmly when Jeremy tried to change it. She told him that she would return to Scarcliff if she couldn't have her Sundays free. Nothing was going to

184

interfere with the time she could have with Marcus. On the rare occasion Marcus was busy and couldn't make it she felt at a loss, and tried not to be jealous, wondering if he was with Fiona. She tried to put Fiona out of her mind, but it wasn't easy.

Sometimes she wondered if she was being silly for not returning home, but something held her back. Marcus tried to persuade her otherwise, and she knew they could see more of each other if she was in Scarcliff, but first she felt she wanted their situation clarified. So far Marcus hadn't said anything about being in love with her. They had spent a lot of time together, they'd kissed and cuddled, they'd talked and teased each other, but . . .

She still wondered about Fiona, and what his relationship was with her. Was she really reading too much into the wonderful weekends they enjoyed? After all Marcus was a good deal older than her. Did he still see her as a liability — a responsibility accepted with good grace? She wished she knew the truth, but was loath to upset the rapport they had.

'What had you in mind for us to do this weekend?' Marcus asked giving her a hug and kiss. It was early Saturday morning and he'd just arrived.

'I wondered about climbing the hill — the one that overlooks the town. I think you're ready for it.'

Marcus groaned. 'Have a heart, Angie love. I'm only here for the weekend. That looks like the north face of the Eiger.'

'Rubbish,' she laughed. 'It will only take us a few hours. We'll be back in time for afternoon tea if we set off straight away. Come on lazy bones.'

Marcus sat down and began pulling on his thick socks and hiking boots, teasing her about how he'd race her to the top. Angeline packed the rucksack with sandwiches and other necessities smiling at how different Marcus was from the stuffy individual she had known in Scarcliff. He was so affectionate and fun-loving. He said he left all his worries behind when he came each weekend, so they refrained from chatting too much about work, and that meant Fiona too, although Angeline would dearly like to know what their relationship was.

They set off along the well trodden path with Angeline leading the way. She set a steady pace and soon they were out on the open fell side. She was finding the going easier this time. She recalled the walk with Russell and recognised how much fitter she was. She wondered what he was doing and whether she would ever see him again. She hoped she would because she would like to thank him for urging her to follow her dream. Part way up the hill they stopped to admire the view and catch their breath.

'It's wonderful here isn't it?' Marcus said flopping down on a boulder and making room for her to sit beside him. 'I can quite see why you stay, young Angie.'

'Hmm. Funny thing though I still miss Scarcliff,' she said. 'I suppose because it's my home town.'

'Scarcliff misses you too.' He playfully tweaked her hair. 'Why not come back next weekend for a change and we can celebrate your birthday there. It will be more appropriate don't you think?'

She smiled thoughtfully. Was he thinking . . . ? 'Yes, all right. I will. I have some things to collect from the house anyway. It will be rather nice to see Scarcliff again. Come on, time we were moving. Those clouds are building up. I wouldn't want to get lost up here, and that can happen if the mist descends, or so I've heard.'

'You sound like quite an authority,' he said, lethargically getting to his feet.

Angeline smiled and hitched her rucksack on her back. 'I came up once with a friend and he told me all about the hazards.'

'A man friend?' Marcus remarked questioningly, his voice sharp causing her to turn towards him.

She was about to tease him but saw how crushed he appeared to be. 'As it happens he was a man,' she said gently. 'A married man, and he was just a friend. Are you jealous?'

He grinned sheepishly pulling her by the hand into the shelter of his arms. He kissed the tip of her nose. 'As a matter of fact yes, dammit, I am. I wouldn't mind getting lost up here alone with you. We could find a cave somewhere and we'd have to snuggle up to keep warm. Wouldn't that be fun?'

'We didn't bring much to eat don't forget,' she laughed, kissing him back. 'A few sandwiches and a couple of bars of chocolate won't last long.'

With humour restored they continued upwards. Marcus often giving her a helping hand when the going got rough. She couldn't get over how jealous he had appeared to be and it gave her a warm inner glow.

They made it to the top where

they celebrated the achievement with a picnic lunch. Fortunately the clouds cleared for a time so they had wonderful views down over the town and the surrounding valley's. Quite a few other walkers arrived shattering their peace so they didn't stay long and returned to Mossdale well satisfied with their outing.

'Shall we eat in or out?' Angeline asked as they wearily scrambled up the stairs of her apartment.

'In,' he chuckled. 'I couldn't walk another step. Your turn to cook I think.'

She pulled a face. 'I'm first for the shower then.'

'Don't take all the hot water then,' he groaned. 'That was some walk. You're a masochist, Angel. I never realised it before.'

★ ★ ★

While Angeline prepared the meal she could hear Marcus singing in the shower cubicle and her thoughts strayed, wondering what he looked like in the nude. She had the strange desire to sneak in and playfully offer to soap his back. She wondered what he'd say if she did. Would he be pleased that she took the initiative or aghast at her effrontery? Their relationship was developing nicely and she wondered whether she ought to suggest he stay the night sometime but didn't want to spoil things.

Each weekend she half expected him to propose and each weekend she was disappointed, and yet she wasn't sure if she would accept if he did. She loved him — in a fashion, and felt comfortable with him, but something was missing and she didn't know what. Some spark of vitality — some fervour — some passion. His kisses — to which she had become accustomed, were pleasant, but not spine tingling. She wasn't sure what love was really meant to be like, but she had the suspicion she hadn't found it yet.

'That looks good.' Marcus appeared in the small galley kitchen smelling wonderfully masculine. She liked it when he wore just a T-shirt and jeans like now. He sneaked his hands round her waist and kissed the nape of her neck. 'You looked miles away. Want to tell me what you were thinking about?'

She blushed and shook her head. 'It was nothing really. It's been a good day hasn't it? Would you care to take the plates and I'll bring the casserole.' What would he have said if she'd admitted her thoughts she wondered, and wished she dare tell him.

★ ★ ★

On Friday morning she packed the car and set off for Scarcliff. She expected to be there by early afternoon. Marcus thought she was arriving on Saturday so she would have a few hours to herself and that suited her. She had contemplated ringing him to tell about her change of plan but decided not to bother him. He would be busy and he was even going to be working Saturday morning he'd told her.

She turned off the motorway and headed for the town feeling strangely apprehensive. The weather was being kind, but a stiffish breeze whisked the leaves from the roadside trees twirling them in the slip-stream. A watery sun shone occasionally from behind the scurrying clouds. It was mild. She liked this time of year. The glorious autumn colours to enjoy before winter set in. Was it right she wondered that one enjoyed best the time of year that you were born? She certainly did.

Approaching the town from the south she drove along the sea front. It was a longer way round to get to her home, but she liked to see the foreshore now that the visitors had gone. She thought about what Jeannie had said, about walking barefoot along the beach and paddling in the sea. She couldn't envisage Sarah doing such a thing. She didn't remember going on the beach often as a child now she came to think of it. Only later when she was old enough to go swimming, then Marcus had taken her a few times. Sarah had been terribly house proud, and grumbled if the wind was in the wrong direction and blew sand in through cracks in the windows and doors.

Angeline stopped for a while and gazed out at the breakwater, recalling the time she had nearly drowned. That was a horrible experience, vividly imprinted on her mind, and one she would never ever forget. She could feel the tug of the current and the water closing over head. She remembered flashing zigzag patterns of light before the welcoming blackness overcame her.

If it hadn't been for Marcus . . . It was only through his swift intervention that she lived to tell the tale. Having seen her from the cliff path, he had run down and dived straight in to pull her to safety. She'd had some explaining to do that day she remembered, and Marcus was never likely to forget it.

She switched on the engine and motored home trying to recall something Marcus told her that day. It was something important he'd told her but for the life of her she couldn't remember. Perhaps she should ask him what it was next time they met, although it was probably some childish pact to get her out of too much trouble.

As she neared her home she had mixed feelings. Should she sell it? That was probably what Marcus would advocate. She was surprised he hadn't already mentioned it. His own house was much smaller and therefore far more economical to run, so she couldn't understand why he was selling it. Was she really considering him as her potential husband? These last few weeks she had the impression that was where they were heading, and yet there was still Fiona.

She turned into the driveway of Viking Lodge, pleased to see the garden looking tidy and still colourful. Terry was a good gardener she had to hand it to him and wondered how he was coping. Had he got himself another job at the supermarket for the winter months? The sum she had agreed with Marcus that Terry should have for keeping an eye on the place wouldn't be sufficient for him to live on. She would like to have paid him more, but Marcus thought she was being over generous as it was since he lived rent free.

Parking the car on the drive she got out and stretched then shivered. There was a nip in the air with the on shore breeze perhaps heralding a sea mist. Quickly unearthing her suitcase she went into the house. All was orderly and tidy but dusty. Someone — it must have been Marcus since he was the only one with a key, had turned the central heating on a low setting so the rooms had the chill off.

She first of all made herself a beaker of coffee letting the vibes of the house settle on her again. It was nice to be back. The old house gave her comfortable feeling. She rinsed out her beaker and then wandered from room to room reflecting on the passage of time and how it made her feel so different about things. She recalled her childhood. Vividly remembering special birthdays, and how often Marcus had been there too.

Had her parents really wanted her to marry him? Was that why they had been thrown together so often? Marcus had always been around, always prepared to make time if her parents asked him to do anything. Why she wondered? What had he hoped to get out of it apart from marrying her — and yet he was still involved with Fiona — wasn't he? She recalled other women he'd been seen with, but they hadn't lasted long, he always returned to Fiona.

She turned up the heating, then pulling on an anorak went for a stroll down the garden before it got too dark. She would like to have gone to see the flat over the garage having heard how much her mother enjoyed working there, but knew that while ever Terry was there she couldn't. Sometime she would have to deal with her father's old Bentley. It might be fun to get it out and take it for a spin before she sold it.

'Well, if isn't the boss lady herself. Come to check up on me have you?' She had been so lost in thought that she hadn't seen Terry behind the hedge.

'Hello, Terry.' She found she could greet him calmly. 'How are things? The garden is looking wonderful. You've done a grand job.'

'Tell that to your foreman then,' he said gruffly leaning on the rake he had been using to collect the leaves off the lawn.

'Marcus?' He wouldn't think much to being called a foreman she thought with a wry smile.

'The bod who keeps poking his nose

in here as if he owns the place, trying to catch me doing something that he can sack me for.'

'Marcus wouldn't . . . he can't . . . '

Terry crossed to the border, taking from his pocket some secateurs, he cut a late flowering rose and handed it to her with a dazzling smile — the same sexy smile which melted her heart. 'I seem to remember the yellow ones were your favourite. How are you, Angie? It's been a long time. Found yourself a boy friend?'

She flushed with embarrassment.

'Gives you lessons like I did does he?' he sniggered. 'You certainly look different. Much more sophisticated with your hair like that, but somehow I preferred you with it long. It looked more unrestrained, wild and sexy.'

Why was it he could turn her bones to jelly? Just seeing him again . . .

'I'm only here for weekend, so if there is anything you need give me a shout.' She turned and headed back.

He called out to her. 'Hey, Angie.

How about that date you always promised me? Now that you are all alone and don't have to conform to what your parents decree, perhaps you'd like to go out with me tonight?'

She turned and stared at him, perplexed. 'Where . . . what had you in mind?' she found herself saying.

'I'm playing a gig at the Spa tonight. Thought you might be interested in seeing how the other half enjoy themselves.'

'Playing? Playing what?' she asked both startled and curious.

'Why don't you come and find out — that is unless you have anything else you'd rather be doing. Call for you at seven.'

He went to put the tools away and Angeline made her way past the summer house heading back indoors. She felt excited. She didn't know why but the thought of going on a date with Terry was exciting. She wondered what he played? Drums probably in a noisy band, she smiled to herself.

Still it was a night out and she could always use ear plugs if it got too wild.

She got ready for her date wondering if the long flouncy skirt — black with embossed pattern and trimmed with delicate lace, and a plain white top was suitable. The Spa was used for all sorts of events, especially after the season ended, from tea dances to full blown orchestral concerts. She hardly thought Terry would be interested in either of those events. She tried twirling her hair into a sophisticated style but it refused to co-operate so she left it loose. Somehow it had been easier to cope with when it was longer she thought, lightly dabbing on make up and some of her favourite perfume.

Terry arrived on the dot of seven looking smart in a casual way. Silky red shirt, slim fitting black jeans and carried a black leather jacket slung over his shoulder. He looked incredibly . . . different. He wasn't the employee gardener tonight, but a suave, nonchalant escort, if perhaps a little on the brash side.

His eyes lit up when she let him in and she blushed under his scrutiny. His eyes travelled from her head to her toes in slow motion before he whistled appreciatively.

'Mighty pretty. Don't forget you're with me tonight. I'm staking my claim. You'd best grab a coat though it gets cold later on.'

She wasn't sure what he was talking about — staking his claim. It sounded double Dutch. 'I thought we'd take the car.'

He pondered for a moment. 'Probably have trouble parking. We're expecting a big turn out.'

'Oh,' she said. 'In that case we'll walk shall we?'

'Got some sensible shoes on?' he asked as she set the burglar alarm.

She grinned. 'I'll put my hiking boots on if you like.'

'Naw, don't bother,' he laughed. 'Another time maybe.'

Being with Terry was fun. He had a way of making her feel special. At times his crude observations and snide remarks caused her to flinch, but on the whole she enjoyed herself.

Angeline wouldn't have believed she could appreciate guitar music, but his playing was inspirational. Apparently the audience thought so too. She wondered what her mother would have thought of it. There were three of them on stage. Terry playing the guitar, Joe the flute and Alan filled in with various instruments. They got a rapturous applause and did many encores before calling it a night at well past eleven o'clock.

'That was marvellous,' Angeline told him as they walked home.

'Think so?' he asked modestly pleased.

'Fantastic. Why didn't you tell me you played the guitar?'

'You never asked.' As they left the promenade he pulled her under a tree and wrapped his arms around her. 'Actually, I'll tell you the truth. I've played musical instruments for many years, but never thought of becoming professional or anything. You started me on the road to stardom.'

'Me?' she frowned. 'How come?'

'I wanted to do something to please you. I knew what you thought of me — the humble gardener. I was all right for the odd kiss and cuddle, but I wasn't good enough as a marriage prospect. So I decided to better myself, and the only way I came up with was with my trusty guitar. Once I settled in the flat I practised for hours on end. I wanted you to be proud of me.'

She smiled. 'You had no need to go to such lengths. I never really got to know you properly, but I always liked you. I got a rude awakening when I saw . . . .'

'I know. You were young and I was randy. You excited me beyond belief, so I had to take my pleasures where I could. You were off limits.' He kissed her and she kissed him back, melting against him, hungry for his kisses.

'You been taking lessons?' he growled.

Pertly she lifted her chin. 'Just grown up,' she remarked dragging him back to the path.

'Angie, is there . . . ? Are you . . . ?'

She was glad it was dark. 'No,' she whispered, not sure if he meant was she still a virgin or was she involved with anyone. 'There's been no-one of consequence.' She thought about Marcus wondering if he would be jealous, if or when he discovered she'd been out with Terry, then thought it would do him good.

'Ready for some more lessons?' he asked with a chuckle, escorting her up the drive and round to the back door.

Angeline had been wondering whether she should ask him in. It was late and she didn't know if he would go when she asked him to. She didn't want things to get out of hand, but decided to take a chance. Ignoring his question she said. 'Fancy a coffee?'

She didn't have to ask twice. He was already following her into the kitchen.

'If that's all you have on offer, then yes please.'

After taking off the alarm she reached in the fridge for a bottle of wine she had bought in specially for Marcus. 'Would you prefer this?' she asked.

He took it from her and read the label. 'Very nice. Expensive. Want me to open it?'

While Angeline located the glasses Terry dealt with the wine, sniffing it appreciatively. Angeline led the way into the library and switched on the electric fire. She uncovered a plate of sandwiches which she had prepared earlier just in case.

Terry stalked about the room, posed aristocratically in front of the fireplace, grinned and then threw himself into her father's old chair. 'Wonderful old house isn't it? Must be worth a packet, what with all these antiques and things. The house at the end of the road sold recently for a small fortune. So what are you going to do with it all, Angie? You're an heiress.'

She didn't really want to discuss it with him. 'I'm not sure,' she said slowly, wondering what he was getting at. 'I'd feel like a traitor if I sold it, and yet it's too big for me. Have you any suggestions?'

He chuckled. 'Nope. Just wondered if that Marcus fellow had got round you. He's itching to get installed here. That's my guess at any rate. I'm surprised he hasn't already asked you to marry him. Snap you up before someone else does.'

She shook her head in disbelief. 'Marcus — here? I shouldn't think so. He's all for looking after his money. He's a solicitor you know and quite wealthy, but he wouldn't throw his money around taking on a place this size. It costs a fortune to run.'

Terry shrugged his shoulders and helped himself to another sandwich. 'Suit yourself, but I know what I know. You mark my words.'

'What's that supposed to mean?'

Terry slouched back in the chair.

'Why does he spend so much time round here then? I'm sure as hell he's not just keeping an eye on me.'

'Does he come here often? There's been no need for Marcus to call round except to check on post, etc.'

Terry gave a knowing smile. 'Brought his lady friend with him sometimes. They didn't see me watching them mind you, but they spent some time here the other week. She looks a bit hoity toity, and certainly wouldn't be my cup of tea. Terribly twee twin set and pearls, sensible pleated skirt, and a snooty look as if everybody else was way beneath her. Can't think what he sees in her — unless she's rich.'

Angeline laughed at his description. There was no doubt about who he was describing. 'Fiona, she's been here too?'

He nodded and leered. 'Yep. Once or twice — mainly evenings.'

'For your information she's his secretary and as far as I know not particularly rich.'

Angeline felt uneasy. She had been building up a rosy picture of marriage to Marcus which was totally false by all accounts.

Sensing her disquiet Terry held out his hand. 'Sorry if I've disillusioned you, sweetheart. Were you and he . . . ?'

She shook her head. 'More wine?'

As she poured some into his glass he snaked a hand round her waist and pulled her down on to his knee. She carefully placed the bottle on the small side table and gave him a playful look of disapproval.

He didn't say anything, but snuggled up to her and she went willingly into his embrace. The past was forgotten.

'Are you happy, sweetheart?'

'Of course. Why shouldn't I be? I've got a home of my own — not this, one in Mossdale. I'm doing what I like doing which is painting, and I'm part owner of an art gallery. Also, I have discovered that my mother is alive and I've been to see her.'

'Good for you. You did it your way

too. You have grown up haven't you?'

'Yes,' she said. 'I didn't want my school friends thinking I was useless. I had to prove to myself that I could cope — find and hold down a job, etc. without help from my parents. I wanted to achieve something I can be proud of so that next time there's a school reunion I shan't feel such a good-for-nothing. I hated school days. I was always the loner — the one they picked on and teased. I wasn't good at anything, and being shy I was an easy target for their hateful pranks.'

'Well now you've something to brag about. You've done it; made something of yourself. So when are you coming home?' he asked as his hands began to wander.

She was having difficulty thinking.

'I've missed you, Angie. It may seem stupid, but I hoped one day you and me . . . you know.'

'No I don't know,' she replied, drawing away from him. How was she to know if what he said about

Marcus and Fiona was true? Indeed why shouldn't Fiona have been with Marcus when he called to see all was well? He was probably giving her lift home and called here on their way. Marcus was an honourable man and wouldn't do anything underhand. She really ought to stop jumping to conclusions.

'What are you getting at?' she asked, trying to ease herself from his grasp.

'Well, I'm keeping my fingers crossed, but I think I've got a tour lined up. America and Canada, and who knows after that. Fancy coming with me?'

She blinked. What was he suggesting?

'You once said you wanted to travel didn't you? We could do whatever you wanted. We could be footloose and fancy free, doing what comes naturally. There's no need to be tied down with bricks and mortar when you have the world at your feet. Surely it's time to live a little. We could make wonderful music, sweetheart. Think of the fun we could have travelling the world. You're a grown woman now. You can make your own decisions, go where you want, and do whatever takes your fancy. I thought I could be your protector. There are lots of wolves out there ready to prey on beautiful, vulnerable young heiresses.'

She blinked again and shook her head as a wave of sadness came over her. Her upbringing hadn't prepared her for the sort of arrangement he had in mind. She wasn't like Jeannie. She couldn't accept the casual lifestyle he was proposing. She wanted to get married and have a family — in the old fashioned traditional manner. She wanted to return to Scarcliff — return to her old school for open day, and be accompanied by a gallant, dashing husband. She wanted to show all her old class mates that she was a success and not a numbskull. She wanted Marcus. She loved him and had done all her life. If necessary she would fight for him, because without him her life would mean nothing. How could she have been so blind?

She shook her head and sighed. Terry probably meant well, but . . . 'I have things to do here. I can't go gadding about the world at the drop of a hat. I'm a business woman. I have a partner to consider. I can't leave Jeremy to do all the work.'

'So it's Jeremy is it?' Terry straightened her top and reached over for his drink. 'Sounds a snob,' he muttered.

'You know nothing about him,' Angeline replied getting to her feet and standing with arms crossed glowering at him. 'He's . . . he is my step-brother actually. You've no right . . . ' She was lost for words.

Terry finished his wine, casually brushed crumbs from his trousers then leisurely got to his feet. 'Best be on my way,' he remarked coldly. 'Marcus may be checking up on you and we wouldn't want your unblemished record to be besmirched would we?'

Angeline saw him out and shot the bolts firmly in place. She was angry.

Angry with herself as much Terry, but what he said was true. She wasn't prepared to lower her standards — the standards her father set admittedly. At school the nuns would have been horrified at what Terry was suggesting so she knew it was wrong for her ever to contemplate going with him. Maybe she could travel the world, she could do whatever she wanted like Terry said, but she knew in her heart that she wanted a man at her side and that man was Marcus.

★ ★ ★

Her birthday celebration was not a huge success. Perhaps she had looked forward to it too much. Angeline had bought a new dress especially for the occasion but when she put it on she wasn't too happy about it. Her hair wouldn't co-operate either, so all in all by the time Marcus called for her she was a trifle fraught.

'Happy birthday, Angie.' He said

bestowing a kiss and presenting her with a neatly tied present. It obviously wasn't a ring, it was too large a packet for that.

'Thank you,' she said trying to sound enthusiastic. The teardrop diamond earrings were splendid and expensive she didn't doubt. She fastened them on and admired them dutifully, but wondered at the same time whether they were his choice or Fiona's.

'I've booked a table at the Pied Piper. Does that suit?'

'Fine,' she said but would have preferred somewhere less chic. The Pied Piper was a large modern establishment, newly opened, and hardly the place for a cosy intimate tête-à-tête by all accounts.

As they drove to the restaurant Marcus looked subdued and thoughtful. Angeline stared through the rain spotted windscreen listening to the swish of tyres on the damp road feeling irrational and irritable. They should have invited Fiona to join them she thought somewhat maliciously, but then wondered if she was getting paranoid about his secretary. Unfortunately she sensed Fiona's presence like a wedge between them.

Finally Marcus said in a somewhat clipped voice. 'I saw lights on last night at Viking Lodge. Did you come back early?'

She nodded and muttered, 'Jeremy suggested I came Friday and stay until Monday so I took him at his word.'

Only the quirk of an eyebrow showed how annoyed he was. 'Why didn't you answer when I rang then?' he snapped.

Angeline bit her lip, to control her annoyance. 'What time was that?'

'About eight o'clock. I happened to be passing. Unfortunately I hadn't the keys with me, and I was taking Fiona home so I couldn't hang about. I saw your car so I rang the door bell but got no response. When I got home I telephoned but still got no reply. Where were you?'

She could have said she was having a bath she supposed. 'Actually I went out last night — with a friend — down on the Spa.'

He frowned and waited for her to explain further so she sighed knowing that he was going to be angry. It was all her fault that the evening was turning into a disaster.

'A trio of musicians were playing. Terry told me about it and he invited me to go with him.'

'You mean you went out on a date with the gardener?' he exploded jabbing at the brakes as the car in front stopped rather suddenly.

She smiled contemptuously. 'How condescending you sound, Marcus. Terry asked me if I'd care to hear him play. It was kind of him I thought, so I went. He's good — very good, but I don't suppose it was in your line. I'd have rung and asked you to go too if I'd thought you would be interested.'

Marcus's face was bleak and only brightened up when she informed him of Terry's forthcoming American tour.

'I'll have to find someone to replace him then,' he remarked with obvious pleasure, and pulled into a vacant slot in the car park.

Angeline decided not to argue with him about it being her responsibility to hire and fire employees. She had already got the evening off to a bad start, and hopefully it couldn't get worse. Unfortunately it could. The restaurant proved to be extremely noisy and the service appallingly slow. Marcus grew more and more irritated, and she was embarrassed beyond belief when he made a scene — remonstrating with the waiter about the food when it finally arrived being cold and the steak under-done. In the end she was glad to leave.

As he unlocked the car he had the grace to apologise. 'I'm sorry, Angie. This isn't the way I intended our evening to go.'

She shrugged her shoulders and strapped herself in. 'It doesn't matter.

It wasn't your fault. We'll know not to go there again in a hurry.'

'Fiona came soon after it opened and highly recommended it.'

She would thought Angeline but said nothing.

Arriving back at Viking Loge she hoped Marcus wouldn't stay long. She felt tired and overwrought but knew he would wish to see her safely indoors as always. In the library he took her father's chair as Terry had done the previous night, but he sat upright and stroked the arms almost lovingly. Angeline watched, fascinated. Marcus cleared his throat and patted his knee to entice her over. Angeline smiled and sat on the rug at his feet and leant against him. It was a peaceful room, the rhythmical ticking of the clock on the mantel piece and the occasional rattle of the window shutters. She felt calmer now. The evening had been a disaster so far, but here in her home she felt at peace.

He stroked her hair. 'There is

something I have been trying to ask you for a very long time, Angie. Tonight I hoped for a quiet, pleasant evening — just the two of us. The Pied Piper was not the right environment — it was a mistake taking you there. Perhaps here though, here is as good a place as any to say what is on my mind.

'I don't suppose it will come as any surprise to you. You know that I am reasonably prosperous and can give you a comfortable life. I . . . would you do me the honour of . . .'

'I'm sorry, Marcus,' she interrupted him rubbing her face against his hand. 'I'm truly appreciative of everything — all you've done for me, but I'm not ready for marriage yet.'

He sat very still and she knew he was offended. 'I promise I'll let you carry on with whatever you wish to do,' he said, picking his words with care, 'but surely it would be better if our relationship was on a formal footing now? After all I've known you a very long time, Angeline and your father led me to believe that he wished me to be his son-in-law. These last few weeks I began to think that you felt the same. I spoke to your father years ago. He thought I should wait until you were twenty-one, and in normal circumstances I would agree with him. However things are different now.'

Angeline couldn't believe what she was hearing. He sounded so cool, almost as if he was offering her a business partnership.

'You need someone to take care of you, Angie. After your father died it was too soon to say anything. I knew I had to let you have some time to find yourself — Fiona was right about that, but now it's time, surely you can see that. After all I'm not getting any younger, and I think I've waited around long enough.'

When Angeline still didn't speak he tried again.

'We would live here and you could have the room over the garage as a workshop to house your painting paraphernalia. I believe you father told me that was what it was used for some time ago. Apparently the light is very good for the purpose.'

Angeline really couldn't believe her ears. Terry had been right. All Marcus wanted was the house — the prestige of living in the grand manner. Probably wanted to announce that he was related to the renown pianist Richard Frost. The more she thought about it the more she realised how snobbish Marcus was, and wondered if he would still be eager to marry her if he knew about Jeannie.

'What about Fiona?' she asked wanting time to marshal her thoughts, even though she wanted to laugh in his face. 'She won't take kindly to you getting married.'

Marcus smiled thinking that she was accepting his proposal. 'She'll get used to the idea.'

'I'm sorry, Marcus but it wouldn't work,' Angeline said getting to her feet to re-fill his glass. 'I've changed. I'm not the same person I was when I left Scarcliff. There are things about me that you wouldn't appreciate.'

'Nonsense. You are still the same charming girl you've always been. You've grown up that's all — grown up into a beautiful young business woman, and I'm proud of you — immensely proud. I guess this has come as a surprise to you, so why don't you sleep on it and I'll call you tomorrow. We can have the day to ourselves, do whatever you want to do. I made a mistake in bringing the subject up tonight. This hasn't been one of our better evenings.'

Like a coward Angeline let him go without telling him again that she couldn't possibly contemplate marriage with him. She hadn't the heart to tell him that she wanted more excitement out of life. She didn't want to become a replica of Fiona — all staid and matronly. She wanted to be loved for herself — not for what she owned.

But she desperately wanted someone

to tame the fire that burned within her. She did so want to know what it was like to go to bed with a man. She was nineteen years old and still naïve about the pleasures of lovemaking. How her school colleagues would laugh if they knew. What other name would they add to the list? What if she was frigid? What am I to do? she wailed in confusion. She wanted Marcus. He was all she ever wanted, but the Marcus she knew in Mossdale — away from Fiona's influence.

* * *

The telephone ringing woke her. Angeline looked at the clock and saw that she had overslept. It was nearly ten o'clock. The wine had dulled her senses and a headache threatened. She reached for her dressing gown and struggled down stairs wondering if it would be a wrong number. It was an ex-directory number so not many people knew it and she couldn't think of anyone who would ring on a Sunday morning — except Marcus.

She felt uncertain about answering, and yet she couldn't bear to hear it ringing and ringing. Her head began to pound — she needed coffee. She was only ever half awake until she'd had her first cup of coffee. Tentatively she reached out and snatched the phone off the hook as if it was something offensive.

'Angeline, it's Jeannie. I'm sorry to bother you, but I'm in terrible trouble and wondered if you could help.'

Her mother was the last person she expected to hear from. Something dreadful must have happened for her to get in touch.

'Of course, Jeannie,' she said plonking herself down on the bottom stair clutching the phone, relieved that it wasn't Marcus. 'What's the problem?'

Her mother sounded extremely agitated, as if she'd been crying.

'I'm . . . I'm in Paris.' After a pause she said, half sobbed. 'I've left Henri.'

For a moment Angeline wondered if she had heard correctly. 'Are you all right?' she asked her head clearing fast.

'Yes, yes dear. I'm fine really I am. I'm sorry, but . . . but I can't get hold of Jeremy. He doesn't answer his phone. A friend will see me to Mossdale . . . and I wondered if it is possible for me to stay with you. I don't like strange hotels, and you were the only person I could think of. Please say if it isn't convenient. I don't want to put you out. I gather you are in Scarcliff.'

'I came home for the weekend. But of course you can stay with me. I'll be happy to have your company. Are you sure you can manage? Would you like me to come an meet you? You could come here to Viking Lodge if you like.'

'No, that's all right. My friend will see me safely to Mossdale. I'll explain everything when I see you. Bless you, my dear. I'm sorry to be such a nuisance.'

After discussions about times she rang off and Angeline wandered into the sitting room and sank down on to the sofa. Her mother — coming to stay at her flat. How could she manage? Jeannie would have to have the bed and she could sleep on the sofa. It converted into a bed, but she hadn't tried it. She must have been psychic she thought. When she had been looking for furniture for her flat she had been going to buy just a couple of arm chairs but she spotted the bed settee and changed her mind. Now she was glad that she had.

She wondered what had happened to cause Jeannie to leave her husband. It must have been something serious, her mother sounded desperate. What if he had discovered Jeannie's past. Had he found out about her? Maybe the servants . . .

She hoped the friend who ever it was wouldn't expect to stay the night too. The flat was only small and she didn't know if it was a man or a woman travelling with Jeannie. It would have been better if they had come to Scarcliff, but she guessed Jeannie wanted to see Jeremy. She would have a bit of explaining to do there.

Angeline stumbled into the kitchen and made some breakfast mentally ticking off what she should take back with her. More sheets and blankets, and she would have to restock her fridge. Thank goodness the supermarket would be open on the by-pass, she could shop there on her way back to Mossdale.

In a flurry of activity she almost forgot to collect the paintings she had promised Jeremy for the gallery. When she was about ready to leave she phoned Marcus. It was a call she was reluctant to make so was thankful to be met by his answering machine. He often left it switched on over the weekends so he wasn't disturbed by clients.

She left a brief message telling him that she had to return to Mossdale urgently and that she would be in touch later in the day. With a last look round she collected her coat and was locking the door when she heard the phone ringing and knew it would be Marcus. She didn't go to answer it.

Terry came from his flat as she was turning the car around on the drive.

'Off back already. I thought you were staying until Monday?'

'Urgent phone call. I'm needed in Mossdale. Sorry can't stop. Good luck with your tour.'

He waved her off and Angeline sighed at what might have been.

# 8

It was late evening when the car drew up. Angeline hurried to help her mother knowing how difficult it would be for her in a strange place for the first time. As she unlocked the shop door she started, recognising a familiar figure in the gloom.

'Russell, what are you doing here?'

He turned on hearing the door opening and they stared at each other, then he gave an embarrassed smile. 'Acting as guide for this lady in distress.' He turned to help Jeannie alight from the passenger seat of his car.

'You two have met before I hear,' Jeannie said grasping Russell's arm. 'I'm so sorry about all this, Angeline. It's very good of you to take me in at short notice. I'll try not to be a nuisance, and as soon as I can contact . . . '

'Don't worry.' Angeline said leading the way upstairs, her mind running riot. She showed them into the sitting room. 'I'll make some tea and then . . . '

Russell seeing her flustered face asked. 'Can I give you a hand, Angie?'

She instantly shook her head. She needed time to compose herself. 'No thanks. Please take a seat. The kettle has boiled, it won't take me long.'

She heard them talking as she prepared the tea and wondered what Russell had told her mother. They would have had plenty of time to talk during the long journey. She carried in the tray and deposited it on a low coffee table beside the settee.

'Thank you for not making a fuss, Angeline,' said her mother. 'I'm sorry if I'm upsetting your plans, but . . . '

'No, it's no trouble, but whatever happened?' She sat next to her mother on the settee dying to know everything, and curious as to how Jeannie knew Russell.

'I'm afraid this is all my fault,' Russell said from the chair opposite.

Angeline's eyes widened. 'You mean you knew my mother all this time?'

He shook his head. 'No. We only met a few weeks ago. I think I told you about the vineyard a friend and I were buying. We bought it from Henri Laporte — Jeannie's husband. Jeannie and I became friendly, more through our love of the Lake District than anything else. I took to calling on her at the chateau, and occasionally stayed for dinner — with Henri too. It was all perfectly civilised.

'To make a long story short, one evening I must have dropped a photograph from my wallet. The one we had taken of the two of us on top of the hill out there,' he said waving in the direction of the window. 'You remember we got that tourist to snap us together for posterity. Anyway it must have slipped down the cushions of the settee and the servants handed it to Henri the next day. Hey presto, it was if world war three had set in apparently.'

'He went berserk,' Jeannie said still sounding shocked. 'He was shouting and bawling, wanting to know the far end of everything. Calling me all sorts of wicked names. Henri honestly thought it was a photograph of me to begin with. I became rather frightened as you can imagine. I guessed it must be of you, Angeline, but I couldn't be sure. Russell hadn't mentioned ever meeting you, but of course there was no reason for him to do so.'

Russell smiled grimly and took up the tale again. 'He brought the photograph round to the place I was staying and demanded to know who the young lady was, and I in my innocence told him. As soon as he heard the name Frost he looked so wild that I knew there was going to be trouble. He demanded to know how old you were, and then stormed away before I had a chance to ask what was wrong. I knew I'd somehow put my foot in it and was afraid for Jeannie. I've never seen a man so incensed.'

'You weren't to know, Russell,' Jeannie said quietly rubbing her hands together. 'Maybe in a way it was for the best. I should have left him long ago, but like a coward I thought I ought be the good little wife and overlook his affairs. At times he even flaunted them, but I felt unable to do anything about it.'

'What did he do next?' Angeline gasped.

'He threatened to come to see you,' her mother said with a sigh. 'In the end I came clean and told him everything. I had to and I was past caring anyway. It was obvious that we couldn't go on living under the same roof. We had a monumental row. I told him how I hadn't seen you since you were a few weeks old, until our secret meeting in Paris. I admitted that he wasn't your father and he obviously deduced you were Richard's daughter.

'After that he became extremely abusive and I really feared for my life. It was far worse than I ever envisaged. So in the end I locked myself in my room and rang Russell. Russell was marvellous. He was already expecting my call apparently. I packed a few things and first thing this morning after Henri had gone to town, Russell came for me. When we got to Paris I rang you from the flat since I could get no reply from Jeremy's number. It was as well I remembered the telephone number for your home at Scarcliff. I was getting worried when I couldn't get hold of either of you.'

'Well at least we'll be able to tell Jeremy the truth now won't we?' Angeline said with a nervous laugh. 'Do you think you will be able to manage staying here? It's only small and of course there are the stairs.'

Jeannie put her hand on her arm. 'I'm so grateful to be back here in Mossdale. I can't thank you enough for having me, and Russell for bringing me. He's been wonderful. I'm so grateful to you both.' She was on the verge of tears.

'Well, ladies I know that you'll have lots to talk about so I'll wish you goodnight, sweet dreams and be on my way. I'm staying at the Royal for the night, but shall I see you both tomorrow?'

Angeline got to her feet to see him out.

Jeannie smiled. 'Thanks again, Russell. You're a true friend. I don't know what I would have done without you.'

'Think nothing of it. I'm delighted to be your white knight and deliver you safely to your daughter's tender care. You couldn't be in better hands, and like I told you before, I'm more then happy to return to Mossdale anytime. Try not to worry. I'm sure we'll be able to work something out.'

Angeline saw him out through the shop and locked the door, breathing deeply as the full impact hit her. What would Marcus say when he heard?

Would his offer of marriage still stand she wondered? Maybe just as well she hadn't accepted his proposal last night. He may wish to rescind it when he hears the facts about her parentage.

'It is only small, do you think you can cope?' she said giving Jeannie a tour of the flat. 'Fortunately I haven't got round to buying much in the way of furniture for you to fall over.'

Jeannie nodded. 'It's perfect. If you find me on all fours though don't be surprised. I do feel guilty for turning you out of your bedroom. Are you sure you won't let me use the settee?'

'I'm quite sure this way is best,' Angeline said firmly. 'If you want anything, anything at all just sing out will you? I think I'd better get washed up and you must be tired after you're long day. Tomorrow is soon enough to go into all the details of what we are going to do next. I really am pleased that you called me you know. I'm beginning to feel more like your daughter.'

Her mother hugged her. 'Bless you. I'll say goodnight then. I hope I haven't spoiled your birthday. Your nineteenth. I never forgot you know. I always wished I could send you cards and presents, but of course I couldn't. Now perhaps I can make up for all those I missed.'

★ ★ ★

Angeline was awake early the next morning and had cleared away the bedding and prepared breakfast before her mother stirred. She was about to take her a cup of tea when Jeannie opened the bedroom door and felt her way to the sitting room.

'Good morning,' Angeline said finding it difficult not to rush to her mother's assistance, but she knew Jeannie would have to learn her way about unaided.

'Good morning, Angeline. Isn't it a beautiful morning. I slept like a log, better than I've slept for literally years. It must be something in the air. I can

238

tell the sun is shining and Mossdale is at it's best, putting on it's autumn overcoat.'

They were having breakfast when Russell arrived.

'Are you going back to France today?' Angeline asked him.

'No. I shall stay for a day or two if you two ladies don't mind.'

They didn't.

'What about your business — the vineyard?'

'My partner, Stephan can handle that. I'm only in as a sleeping partner you know. I put up most of the money but he supplies the know how. I do believe he's happier when I'm not around poking my nose in everywhere and asking stupid questions.'

Jeannie laughed. 'You can be my eyes and describe the scene out there,' she said turning to face the window. 'It feels good to be back. I've missed it.'

'I expect you can picture it all quite well,' Russell replied affectionately covering her hand with his. 'It's like your paintings. Beautiful blue sky, fluffy white clouds skirting the tops of the hills, and golden burnished bracken.' Turning to Angeline he said. 'What a stroke of luck finding this place. Have you been in business long? The gallery downstairs looks wonderful.'

'I found this the day after you left, but since then I've become a partner with Jeremy at the Laporte Gallery so the shop downstairs is a sideline.'

'Fantastic. I told you you would go far. No young man on the horizon yet then?' he grinned mischievously.

'Well . . . '

'Oh, so there is. Tell all, young lady.'

Jeannie pricked her ears up.

Angeline decided it needed clarification. 'Marcus, my friend from Scarcliff asked me to marry him this weekend as a matter of fact.'

Russell raised an eyebrow.

Angeline shrugged her shoulders. 'I don't know. I thought I did but now I'm not sure.'

'You're not exactly an old maid,

Angie. I should take your time if I were you.'

'He is someone I've known all my life but he is rather sombre at times — something to do with being a lawyer I suppose. Anyway I said I'd think about it. He wants me to pack up and return to Scarcliff.'

'From the tone of your voice you don't sound madly keen.'

She shook her head. 'I'm not ready to go back yet. Soon maybe but not yet.'

'I've got some good news,' said Russell. 'I've got my old flat back. I went round before coming here this morning, and now that the season is drawing to a close the landlord was glad of a tenant.'

'So you'll be staying a while,' they said in unison.

Russell looked pleased. 'As long as you need me. I rang Stephan and he said not to hurry back.'

'What will Henri do?' Angeline asked. 'Once he found you'd gone,

Jeannie? Do you think he'll come after you?' She didn't fancy having an irate man turning up on her doorstep and Henri sounded uncontrollable.

Jeannie shook her head. 'I shouldn't think so. He'll probably think it's good riddance and seek solace in the arms of one of his myriad lady loves. I never let on that I knew about his affairs, but Jeremy found out and that was one of the reasons for him leaving.'

At that moment Jeremy arrived, bounding up the stairs two at a time. He burst into the room and stared at the occupants for a moment speechless. 'Mother,' he said with a strangled cry. 'What are you doing here?'

Jeannie flinched at the tone of his voice. 'I've left your father,' she said simply.

'Why? What happened? Why didn't you ring me? How did you get here?' Jeremy threw question after question clearly annoyed for not being informed earlier.

'Calm down,' said Russell. 'Your

mother's had a trying ordeal.'

'Who are you?' demanded Jeremy crossly. 'What's it to do with you? I was talking to my mother if you don't mind.'

'Please, Jeremy,' interrupted Jeannie. 'Let me explain. I did try to contact you on the telephone, but there was no answer. That was why I rang Angeline.'

'I was out most of yesterday,' Jeremy admitted sulkily.

'A girl friend?' his mother queried.

'As a matter of fact it was, but that still doesn't . . . '

'All in good time, son. I have some news which you may find difficult to accept. Won't you sit down.'

Jeremy scowled but took the proffered seat.

Russell and Angeline decided it was time to leave mother and son alone together. 'I'd like to have a look round downstairs if I may?' Russell said diplomatically.

Angeline volunteered to show him. As they were leaving the room they overheard Jeannie gently telling Jeremy who Angeline really was.

Jeremy looked shell shocked when he joined them a short while later and was in a very subdued mood. 'You should have told me,' he snapped at Angeline.

'Jeannie asked me not to,' she replied. 'She didn't want any of this to ever come out. She didn't want to hurt you — or your father.'

They trouped back to rejoin Jeannie.

'Jeremy says his flat isn't suitable for me,' Jeannie said.

'There are far too many awkward stairs and the balcony overhangs the lake,' Jeremy tossed in almost angrily. 'I wouldn't want you to fall in there.'

'So it's best if she stays here,' Angeline said quietly.

Jeremy slowly nodded his agreement. 'For the time being at least. I'll look around for alternatives as soon as possible.'

Russell sensed tension. 'If you are ready, Jeannie, I promised to take you out today, remember? Let's go and find all those old haunts of yours and give these youngsters time to themselves. This is a working day for them.'

Left alone Jeremy and Angeline stared at each other both feeling awkward.

'I hope it isn't too much of a shock?' Angeline said eventually, beginning to clear the breakfast table.

Jeremy walked over to the window, his hands deep in his pockets — a familiar stance. 'I can't somehow believe . . . Why didn't she say something before? She could have told me. I would have understood. I've always stuck up for her.'

Angeline handed him a beaker of coffee. 'I think she was feeling terribly guilty and stayed with your father out of loyalty and remorse. I don't know your father, but from what she told me she went in fear of him.'

He turned. 'So where does that leave us?'

'As far as I am concerned it makes no difference whatsoever. We are still partners and Jeannie is welcome to stay with me as long as she likes. I still have the house in Scarcliff which would probably be more suitable, but we'll have to see how things develop. The break from your father has been traumatic so she needs time to settle down before making any major decisions.'

Jeremy accepted the situation with remarkable resilience Angeline thought. She had been afraid when he learned that his mother was not the pillar of society he had always believed, he might be extremely angry. He idolised her and to find that she had behaved disgracefully would hit him hard.

After he left Angeline rang Marcus. She hadn't had time the previous evening — or at least hadn't felt able to bring herself to ring and explain what had happened. It wasn't the sort of thing one discussed over the phone. This time Marcus himself answered which was most unusual. Fiona fended calls quite fiercely as a rule. He didn't sound too pleased.

'Angeline. I waited patiently for you to call last night. What's happened? You said it was complicated.'

'Yes, Marcus it is. I can't very well explain over the phone, but I wondered if you were coming over again next weekend.'

There was a moment's pause before he asked if it would be worth his while.

Angeline angered by his implication snapped. 'If you just want an answer to your 'proposal' then no it wouldn't be worth your while. I'm sorry Marcus but I really think you ought to marry Fiona. She's obviously dying to be the next Mrs Stone and she will make you an admirable wife.'

She slammed the phone down, furious with him for his high handedness. Who did he think he was? Or for that matter did he really believe her father would arrange a marriage without considering her feelings? Well she was glad that was sorted out. So why was she crying?

# 9

The next few days were busy ones for Angeline. She spent as much time as she could with her mother, getting to know her better and helping her come to terms with the breakdown of her marriage as best she could. Fortunately Russell helped a great deal and the three of the spent some pleasant hours together. It helped take her mind of her own problems, but there were times when she wished she could escape.

By Friday morning, since Angeline hadn't heard any more from Marcus she assumed he wouldn't be coming for the weekend and she was bitterly disappointed. She had hoped they could have remained friends and perhaps, given time maybe be more than just friends . . . Her feelings were in a state of flux.

Russell and her mother went out for

the day and Angeline was in the shop helping out when the phone rang. It was Marcus, the bearer of bad news — nothing too serious he hurriedly allayed her worst fears. 'There's been a fire at Viking Lodge — restricted to the garage and studio I'm relieved to say. I know it's no longer your responsibility but I thought you ought to know.'

'A fire? How did it start? Is there much damage? Was Terry there? What do you mean no longer my responsibility?'

'The fire broke out in the studio above the garage. Much of that block has gone. Fortunately I managed to drive your father's Bentley out before the flames got to it.'

'Is Terry all right?'

'Oh yes, he's fine,' Marcus remarked scornfully.

Angeline sensed there had been conflict between them. 'I'll drive over and see for myself,' she told him.

'There's no need . . . '

'I'll come anyway.'

'What time should I expect you?'

'I can't leave straight away so it will be early evening I suppose. I take it the fire is out and the main part of the house hasn't been damaged?'

'Correct,' he snapped. 'I'll see you later. Drive carefully.'

Angeline wearily put down the phone. What had been going on? From the tone of his voice she deduced Marcus blamed Terry for the fire. Marcus had never liked him and would lay the blame at his door if he possibly could. She immediately contacted Jeremy and told him what had happened.

'You will tell Jeannie that I'm sorry not to be here when they get back won't you?

'Don't worry, you go and see the damage for yourself. Leave mother to me.'

Angeline threw an overnight bag in the car and set off. All went well for the first part of the journey — she was making good progress until she had to stop for petrol. There was a café attached to the filling station so she pulled in for a sandwich and a coffee. She hadn't meant to spend long there, but when she returned to her car it refused to start.

After much cursing she returned to the filling station and asked for their assistance, but there was only a young girl in charge of the till and no mechanic. It seemed like several hours before she managed to procure one from the nearest town, and after a few minutes poking around under the bonnet he got it started.

It was very late by the time she arrived in Scarcliff. For some reason she still half expected to see fire engines and lots of people everywhere, but all was quiet as the grave. She parked her car behind the Bentley on the drive and walked round to the back of the house to view the garage block. The security lights flashed on and the sight that met her eyes was far worse than she'd envisaged. The whole of the roof had gone, and charred timbers showed like ribs of a discarded carcass. Part of the original stable block walls still stood all blackened and disfigured. Wisps of powdery grey ash whirled around in the chilly breeze and she shivered.

The kitchen door opened and Marcus strode over towards her. 'Sickening isn't it?'

She nodded too distressed to answer. She had been thinking she would bring Jeannie to see round her old studio one day, now it was a ruin.

'Better come inside before you catch your death of cold,' he murmured pulling her gently towards the house. 'There's nothing you can do about it now. You're later than I expected. Did you have problems?'

'How did it happen?' she asked doing as he suggested and walked into the kitchen.

'Your watchdog didn't do a very good job,' Marcus growled.

'Terry? How come?'

'Come and sit down and I'll tell you

all about it. I've just made a fresh pot of coffee.'

They went into the library. Marcus had already switched on the electric fire. He had obviously been working there, his papers were spread about the coffee table. He collected them together as Angeline went to warm her hands. Marcus sat back in her father's chair.

'Do you need a brandy instead, you're as white as a ghost?' he asked scrutinising her face.

'No,' she replied subsiding into a chair on the other side of the fireplace. 'Coffee's fine. Just tell me what happened.'

He sighed. 'I told your father that I didn't trust that gardener, but he felt he ought to give the fellow a chance. You know what he was like, saw good in everyone.'

Angeline frowned wondering what on earth Terry had done.

Marcus continued. 'Last night soon after I arrived home I spied various disreputable looking individuals making their way surreptitiously towards the garage apartment. They looked an uncouth lot, and I knew there was going to be trouble.'

The word *home* made Angeline blink. Did he view Viking Lodge as his home already? She let him carry on with his narrative, but knew she had to take him to task over his arbitrary manner in taking up residence in her house.

'I immediately went looking for your employee gardener,' he growled, 'to have it out with him. After a great deal of difficulty I discovered him in the summerhouse. He was not alone. To put it mildly, we had a few words and he became abusive and violent. I gave him his marching orders pronto, and when I mentioned that I thought he ought to have some regard for his wife and family he took a swing at me.'

'He's married?' Angeline said in astonishment.

'Oh yes, he's married all right, and

has two children whom he's deserted.'

'But he said he was homeless. That was why father let him have the flat.'

'Yes I know, but I made enquiries. Anyway I left him grovelling on the ground hardly able to stand. Heaven knows what they had been drinking or taking. I'd said my piece and hoped they would clear off. I couldn't remain to see they left as I had an appointment in town I couldn't afford to miss.

'I heard the fire engines racing past my office, and sixth sense told me that they were heading here. When I arrived smoke was billowing from the end of the outbuildings farthest from the house, so I thought it prudent to get the car out of harms way.'

'What about Terry?' she asked, more concerned for human life than possessions.

'Oh, he had already left. High tailed it as soon as the fire started I gather. You'll not see him again if he's got any sense. Does that bother you?'

She shrugged her shoulders.

'Are you staying here tonight?' he asked.

'Yes, of course. Surely I don't need permission to sleep in my own house! And there's no need for you to stay,' she replied haughtily. 'I'm perfectly happy here on my own you know.'

'That's as maybe but I'm staying. I knew you weren't listening when I informed you about your father's will.'

'What . . . what do you mean? What are you getting at?'

'Simply that this is my house, Angel. I've owned it for a good few years.'

'But . . . but . . . '

'My ancestors built this house, but my grandfather was a spendthrift and by the time my father took over, the debts were too much for him to keep possession. That was something which he always regretted to his dying day, and I vowed that one day I would buy it back. Yes, Angel, I know what you thought. You thought I wanted to marry you to get my hands on it didn't you?'

'I . . . I didn't think anything of the sort.' She could feel her cheeks flame with the lie.

'Funny,' he remarked, 'because that is what Terry told you isn't it? He's been putting his oar in all the way along hasn't he? What, I'd like to know is what you really think, Angeline — now that you are an adult — a fully grown up woman in all senses of the word.'

She didn't like the tone of his voice. It had a cynical twist to it as if he knew some secret. The fact that he owned the house though was a blow to her pride. She had always imagined returning to live there. For the moment she pretended to overlook what he had said. Rising to her feet she glanced at the clock as it struck ten.

'I've had a tiring week so I'll say goodnight. Thank you for all that you have done, Marcus. I am grateful. I'm somewhat confused by what has happened and what you've told me, but I think it would be best if we continued this conversation in the morning. My head is spinning.'

His mouth twisted in a wry smile. 'I'll bring you up a couple of aspirins.'

'No . . . that won't be necessary,' she stammered and hurried from the room.

Ten minutes later he tapped on her door and entered before she had time to call out.

'Your pills and a glass of warm milk,' he murmured bearing a tray. He was already in his dressing gown prepared for bed himself.

'Thank you,' she managed as he placed the tray on the bedside table. She smiled weakly but her smile turned to astonishment as he proceeded to take off his dressing gown.

'What are you doing?' she asked huddling under the covers, her voice quavering with nervousness.

'Coming to join you,' he remarked quite casually as if it was the most normal thing in the world.

'But . . . but you can't. Go find yourself another bed.'

'But I like this one, Angie sweetheart. Don't tell me you are shy. Not after all the lessons Terry has been giving you. Oh yes, I've heard all about your loving relationship with the hired help. There was me thinking what a simple, innocent, naïve young woman you were, and that I should wait a while before introducing you to the joys of the bedroom. Maybe you prefer it in the summer house or down in the long grass, but I definitely prefer it inside. I prefer subdued lighting, soft music and a drop of wine. It improves the mood no end — although perhaps you already know that. Maybe you could teach me a thing or two.'

'Marcus, please,' she gazed at him imploringly.

'Begging me now are you? Want to find out from a more civilised man what you're missing — what you could have had a long time ago if I hadn't been such a gentleman.'

'No, please,' she cried, 'You don't understand.'

'Oh but I do, my sweet angel. I understand perfectly what has been going on for these past two years. Having spoken to your father I was prepared to wait until you were twenty-one before asking you to marry me, under the misguided impression that a carefully brought up young woman like you would still be a sweet innocent virgin on our wedding day. It's apparently too late for that, so it's no good resorting to recriminations and tears, because I don't care any more. I am quite prepared to stay with you tonight though. I wouldn't want you to be lonely, and it is feasible that Terry could come creeping in. I could do to finish what I started with that vermin.'

Angeline reached across for the glass of milk, pretended to drink, then threw it in his face and dashed for safety. She made it as far as the door before he recovered, only to discover that he had locked the door and removed the key.

'I might have known you would do

that,' he remarked coldly.

Angeline turned to face him knowing that her only means of escape was to placate him and that would be no mean feat after what she had done.

'Marcus, please will you listen to me?'

He sat on the bed moping his face with a handkerchief. Cautiously she approached the opposite side of the bed, conscious of her skimpy night-dress. Why oh why hadn't she put on some pyjamas she thought, instead of the shortest night-dress she possessed. She pulled at the counterpane in an effort to hide her near nakedness.

'I don't know what Terry told you, but I can tell you with my hand on my heart that . . . that I haven't . . . what I mean is Terry and me . . . we didn't . . . you know what I mean.' She finished miserably.

He stared at her for several agonising moments, clearly trying to comprehend. 'Is that true?' he barked.

She backed away when he made a

move towards her. She nodded. 'Yes,' almost sobbing with relief that he believed her. 'Yes, it's true. I wouldn't lie to you, Marcus. You always said you knew when I told a lie.'

He said no more, merely dug in his pocket for the door key, went across, unlocked it and walked out. At the last minute he turned. 'I'll bid you good night, Angeline. I'll see that you're not disturbed. We'll talk in the morning.'

When he'd gone she flung herself on the bed and cried her eyes out.

★ ★ ★

The phone rang before she was properly awake. She was about to get out of bed when she heard Marcus speaking to someone and assumed he'd answered it. Thinking it maybe for him anyway she settled back under the covers. She wasn't looking forward the their next meeting and wished to put it off for as long as possible. The next minute he tapped on her door.

'Angeline, are you awake? You're wanted on the telephone. Someone called Jeannie.'

Angeline threw back the duvet and hastily grabbed a dressing gown. 'My mother,' she said hurrying past Marcus and down the stairs. She was half way to the phone when she realised what she had said. She gave him a quick backwards glance hoping he hadn't heard, but from the expression on his face he had.

'Hello, Jeannie,' she said pouncing on the handset. 'Are you all right? I presume Jeremy told you what happened.'

'Yes, of course, dear. We were wondering how you were. I'm terribly upset to hear about the fire. Is there much damage?'

Angeline didn't know how best to tell her without it sounding brutally frank. 'I'm sorry to say your old studio took the brunt of it.'

'Oh dear, I am sorry.' There was a pause. 'Russell suggested we had a run over to Scarcliff and see if we can help in any way. Would you mind?'

'No, I'd be delighted,' Angeline said, thinking that it would make things easier all round. She still had to face Marcus. 'We've plenty of rooms you know,' she added thoughtlessly. 'Pack an overnight bag and we'll expect you in time for lunch.'

Marcus was busy in the kitchen preparing breakfast when she entered. She wondered if he had overheard her invitation and whether he would be annoyed.

'Mother?' he queried lifting an eyebrow enigmatically. 'This Jeannie is your mother? How come?'

She nodded and went to get the orange juice from the fridge and poured herself some. For some reason her mouth felt very dry. As she put the glass down Marcus took hold of her by the wrist. 'Are you going to explain?' he growled, 'or do I have to shake it out of you?'

Snatching herself loose she calmly

went to sit at the table and methodically helped herself to some cereal. Having carefully poured on the milk she picked up a spoon, but then paused. She replaced the spoon and clasped her hands together, rubbing them nervously. Better get it over with she thought, unless she wanted ulcers.

'A short while ago I discovered that my mother was still alive.' She didn't dare look in his direction, but now that she had started she wanted to get it off her chest. Marcus said nothing. He stood with arms crossed leaning against the kitchen sink, and since he obviously wasn't going to interrupt she continued. 'Until recently she — that is my mother, Jeannie Laporte lived in Paris, but last weekend she came to stay at my flat in Mossdale — she's left her husband.'

Having given him the brief facts Angeline deliberately picked up her spoon and began eating her cereal, trying to give the impression that she was calm, and hiding her depression quite well. Why was it that everything should go so wrong all at once?

The toaster popped up and Marcus went to retrieve the lightly browned toast casually remarking, 'So that was why you went haring back to Mossdale. Why didn't you tell me?' He didn't sound astonished or embarrassed, or in anyway put out, except for her not confiding in him.

She felt guilty for not doing so. Marcus had always been there for her, she owed him a lot. 'I was going to — at the next opportunity,' she replied quickly averting her gaze from his studious inspection. 'That was why I asked if you were coming to see me. I didn't think it the sort of thing to spring on you, especially after . . . after your . . . after last weekend. I couldn't discuss it over the phone. I didn't know what to do.'

Marcus poured them both some coffee and sat down opposite her. 'Would you care to begin at the beginning and tell me all that's been going on?' His voice was silky with the hint of disapproval.

Angeline sighed. What did it matter now? What did any of it matter? She would have to find her own way in the world as she had planned to do anyway, so she began at the beginning and told him everything. He listened quietly without interrupting, munching toast in an unconcerned manner. When she finished and sat back waiting for his verdict, he smiled and reached out to take her hands in his. He stroked them tenderly and shook his head from side to side.

'So where does that leave us, Marcus?' she asked, her heart in her mouth. She wanted his approval — just as she always had. Now that she was about to lose everything she realised that without a doubt she loved Marcus and would do so until her dying day. He might not be exciting or witty, but he was always so understanding and courteous towards her, and always had her best interest at heart.

She wanted to rush into his arms and tell him all that he meant to her. She wanted to tell him openly and honestly that she truly loved him, but the words wouldn't come. They stuck in her throat, fearful that too much damage had been done. After all, he might still believe all that Terry had boasted about, whatever that may have been. She looked across him with sad tear filled eyes.

'I'm not sure . . . ' he began, but was interrupted by the phone again. This time it was Fiona for him. When he returned he said he had to go but that he would be back later and they could continue their discussion. 'Keep the door locked, and if you catch sight of Terry let me know.'

★ ★ ★

Angeline was glad when Russell and her mother arrived. It meant that discussions with Marcus would have to wait a while. Perhaps with a lapse in time he might accept that she was innocent of all charges, except she had not confided in him. The misunderstanding over who owned Viking Lodge was something which had taken her completely by surprise, and took some getting used to. It was her home — the only home she had known. She wouldn't want Marcus to marry her because of some sort of pact with her father. Why had her father sold it to him? Why hadn't she been told?

* * *

They were all out in the back garden — Jeannie, Russell and Angeline, observing the damage to the garage when Marcus returned, much later than expected. Angeline made the introductions.

'How about us going out for a spot of lunch and get to know one another?' Marcus suggested glancing at his watch. 'I only discovered this morning that I had a future mother-in-law. Perhaps I ought to ask your permission to marry your daughter?'

Jeannie chuckled. 'I think perhaps we had better get acquainted. Angie didn't tell me things had progressed so far. I suspect she hadn't got round to telling you that I don't see too well, although strangely enough this last week I have the feeling that my eyesight is improving.'

'Jeannie, that's wonderful news,' Angeline said thinking it was about time she found her voice. Marcus had floored her with his insinuation. She didn't recall having agreed to marry him. She remembered last night his derogatory tone in which he'd made it plain that he wouldn't entertain her as a wife at any price. Perhaps this mornings talk had paved the way . . . Was it his way of protecting her from scandal?

She frowned in his direction. He smiled back and drew an arm around her waist proprietarily. 'Don't I get a welcome kiss?' he murmured and without waiting for her to respond, his lips descended claiming hers demonstratively. She shivered with . . . with surprise and a thrill of joy rippled through her.

Blushing furiously she stared into his face wondering what his intentions were regarding her. She frowned questioningly.

'My poor Angeline, you look so enchanting when you blush,' he said in an undertone. 'I suggest we all retire to the Wagon & Horses and get better acquainted.' Turning his attention to Jeannie and Russell he enquired if they would care for a spot of lunch. He explained that the place he had in mind would be quiet, and assured Jeannie that she would not feel uncomfortable.

'We can't all get into my car or yours, Russell, so how about if you follow us? I want a few words in private with Angeline about something that cropped up earlier. We can talk on the way to the restaurant.' He led her away, masterfully organising them, seemingly stamping his authority.

They had hardly left the driveway when he forestalled her many questions. 'I know what you are going to say so I'll say it for you shall I? You don't know how I have the temerity to infer that we are to be married. But you know, sweetheart — you have always known that it was inevitable. You can't resist my magnetism — my wonderful charisma.' He chuckled. 'I suppose to one as young as you I appear staid and unadventurous. All I can say in my defence is that I have been waiting for the right moment.

'I wanted to tell you — show you, years ago how I felt about you, but your parents felt it inappropriate. They viewed you as a child, to be protected by them while ever they lived. When your father died, and after a discreet interval I felt I could sound you out, so you took the wind out of my sails when you upped and left Scarcliff. I tried to be philosophical. You'd had such a restricted life and it was probably best you had a taste of freedom. In my own mind I was certain that the bonds that held us together — bonds that I hope I haven't been imagining, would make us strong enough to survive.

'I must admit I was lonely once you left Scarcliff and I threw myself into work, trying not to worry about you, but I was glad of an excuse — any excuse to go to Mossdale to see for myself. In a way I hoped you would find the outside world too complex and disturbing, and that you would soon return to the fold, so I have to hand it to you, you proved to be remarkably resilient. I'm proud of you — proud of all that you have achieved, and will be exceedingly grateful if you will agree to be my wife. Please dispel from your mind any thought of there being any coercion in any form. I believe that now we can be honest with each other, I can show you how different I am from the serious person you see me as.'

Angeline was taken aback. 'You . . . you

really do love me? And you want to marry me — even knowing everything,' she whispered, still only half believing what she was hearing.

'Oh yes, sweetheart and the sooner the better. I believe I have been patient long enough. Besides,' he chuckled, 'your mother is well aware that I stayed the night — all night. And we were completely alone, Angie. What do you think she's thinking?'

Angeline stared at him, at first belligerently and then smiled when she saw that he was teasing her. 'But nothing happened, and nothing is going to happen until I get a few things sorted out.' She wasn't going to be bamboozled any more. They had things to talk about, but unfortunately they were running out of time as Marcus steered the car into the pub car park.

'After lunch shall we go for a walk along the beach,' he said depositing a light kiss on her cheek. 'We can talk there without interruption. Except perhaps for the odd kiss or two along the way of course. I've some catching up to do. Come along and let's see to our guests.'

Marcus was in sparkling form during lunch and she had to laugh at his witty approach. He captivated Jeannie, making sure she didn't feel uneasy with the strange surroundings. Angeline had never seen him so talkative and sociable.

# 10

After lunch as promised, while Jeannie and Russell took a turn around the house and gardens Marcus took Angeline along the cliff top. Even though the sun was shining it was cold out so they walked briskly to begin with until they were clear of the many dog walkers who found the cliff tops an ideal place to exercise their animals. By unspoken agreement Marcus led her to the place at the point just below the skyline. There was a large flat stone which made a superb seat from which to admire the view. Scarcliff looked magnificent with the wide sweep of the bay being washed by the incoming tide.

They sat side by side watching the waves crashing over the rocks, each thinking their own private thoughts. Finally Marcus pulled her into the shelter of his arms and kissed the tip of her nose. 'Now my love,' he said with a wry grin. 'What great mysteries are there yet to unfold? What is it that is bothering you?'

'First will you explain how my parents came to be living in your house?'

'No problem. The story begins many years ago with my great grandfather. He was a builder — a successful builder, and he built Viking Lodge for his family. He had one son who carried on the family firm, but unfortunately wasn't so astute as his father. He found himself in difficulties and tried to gamble his way out of trouble. As one would expect it didn't work and he had to sell the house to pay off his debts.

'He in turn had a son — my father, who as you probably know was an architect. He was good at his job and hoped one day to buy back Viking Lodge in memory of his ancestors. Unfortunately he died before he could do so. As it turned out my father and your father became great friends and I became a frequent visitor to your home after my mother died. Your parents treated me like a son for which I was eternally grateful.

'I was nearly twelve years old when you arrived. At first I was somewhat put out at the intrusion I must say. I was used to having their undivided attention and now here was this tiny scrap of a baby who gave great concern. They fussed over you like you were the crown jewels and I resented it. When I saw how worried they were about you though I too became concerned. I didn't want you to die — I wanted you to live and be my sister.

'As you grew up I became more and more aware of a close bond with you, but it wasn't a brotherly sort of love. I knew from a very early age that I wanted to marry you and take care of you forever. The difference in our ages could be overcome — with patience on my part, and I know that your father was delighted at the prospect.

'When your father had to stop working I learned that they were going to have to find somewhere else to live. They couldn't afford to maintain such a large property on their diminished income. So I stepped in and offered to buy the house, but let them live in it. From my point of view the arrangement was ideal. The house was far too big for me to look after on my own, and I still had my own place in any case, which as you know has proved difficult to sell in this depressed market. I saw it as a way of keeping in touch with you, and also helping out old friends who had been very good to me in the past. Your parents were proud people and I hated to think of them living in reduced circumstances at their time of life.'

'They loved the house — as I do too,' Angeline said. 'I'm sorry if I got the wrong end of the stick. It was silly of me to think you wanted to marry me because of the house. So why do you want to marry me? I'm not pretty, I'm not intelligent, and I'd be hopeless entertaining your business clients. Fiona would be far better at all those things than me.'

'Oh, my wonderful, Angel. Why do you think I want to marry you? Because I love you of course. I always have done, ever since I saved you from drowning out there. I knew then what my fate was to be. I wanted always to be there to take care of and cherish you. I suspect you have forgotten the pledge I made you all those years ago.'

She frowned. 'Pledge?'

'I see I'll have to remind you. After I dragged you from the water you remonstrated with me, and told me in no uncertain terms that I ought to have let you drown. You were upset by something one of the girls at school had said — about you being illegitimate. Now do you remember?'

She shook her head. The whole episode was something she had wanted to forget.

'You told me quite miserably that nobody would ever want to marry you, and that you didn't want to live. So I made you a promise there and then that I would wait until you were old enough and I would marry you. Not because nobody else would want to I hasten to add, but because I loved you my adorable girl. I've been amazed at your dedication and courage under trying conditions, and as for not being beautiful, I think you are extraordinarily well named, my Angel. You bring a wonderful glow to my heart just being with you. You're so stunningly attractive, and if you'll marry me I'll be the happiest man alive.'

She stared at him in amazement. 'I don't understand . . . '

'It's quite simple. I made you a promise and I intend to keep it. I trust you won't renege on our agreement. We were to get engaged on your birthday, and to set your mind at rest about Fiona. Maybe she is a good secretary, and maybe she can cook and entertain clients, but I have no wish to marry someone with such a cold personality. I want a warm loving woman to grace my bed — that comes first and foremost in my book.

'The other attributes — they can come later if you feel the need to participate in those quarters,' he laughed. 'Now I see I have made you blush again. I'm not really so serious all the time you know. Out of business hours I'm sure we'll be able to find lots of ways to please each other that we'll both find enjoyable. I'm sorry if I came on strong last night. I believed what that rogue Terry told me, so you can imagine how I felt.'

'There never was anything between us apart from friendship,' she said nibbling her bottom lip. 'My mind is hazy about what happened the time I nearly drowned, but I do know that you have always been my protector, and yet I never knew why.'

'I know the real Angeline. I know

that underneath that shy reserve there is a passionate nature waiting to be unlocked. I want to be the man to unlock it, my love. For my part, since that day, I have always accepted that we were betrothed, so will you marry me?'

Angeline threw her arms round his neck and kissed him. 'Yes please,' she whispered.

## THE END

*Other titles in the*
*Linford Romance Library:*

## TO LOVE IN VAIN

### Shirley Allen

When her father dies in a duel, Anna has no money to pay off his debts and is thrown into Newgate Gaol. However, she is freed by her cousin Julien, who takes her to her grandparents in France. Finding herself surrounded by people she cannot trust, Anna turns more and more to the handsome, caring Patrick St. Clair. Then, to her horror, she discovers her guardians are planning her marriage to a man of their choosing!

# DREAM OF A DOCTOR

## Lynne Collins

Melissa had discarded a sentimental dream of the attractive doctor who had inspired her to train as a nurse. However, his unexpected return to the hospital meant that she was constantly reminded of a fateful weekend. And so was Luke, for very different reasons. Time hadn't healed the damage done to his heart by her beautiful cousin, Julie, who Melissa knew he still loved. So it would be foolish to allow a dream to be revived when it could never come true.

# SHELTER FROM THE STORM

## Christina Green

Kim takes a job on Dartmoor, trying to hide from her unhappy past. Temporarily parted from her son, Roger, and among unfriendly country neighbours, Kim finds the loneliness of the moor threatening, especially when her new boss's girlfiend, Fiona, seems to recognize her. Again, Kim runs. But Neil, her employer, soon finds her. When Kim discovers that he, too, has a shadow in his past, she stays on at Badlake House, comes to terms with life, and finds happiness.

# A SUMMER FOLLY

## Peggy Loosemore Jones

Philippa Southcott was a very ambitious musician. When she gave a recital on her harp in the village church she met tall, dark-haired Alex Penfold, who had recently inherited the local Manor House, and couldn't get him out of her mind. Philippa didn't want anything or anyone to interfere with her career, least of all a man as disturbing as Alex, but keeping him at a distance turned out to be no easy matter!

# IMPOSSIBLE LOVE

## Caroline Joyce

When Maria goes to live with her half-brother on the Isle of Man, she finds employment as a lady's maid to the autocratic Mrs. Pennington. Maria finds herself becoming very attracted to the Penningtons' only son, Daniel, but fights against it as he is from a different class. She becomes engaged to Rob Cregeen, who takes a job in the Penningtons' mines. But when Rob is killed in a mining disaster, Maria blames the Penningtons . . .

# THE DARK DRUMS

## Anna Martham

Anona Trent is engaged by Jermyn St Croix as governess to his daughter at his plantation home on the island of Saint-Domingue in the Caribbean. At Casabella, Anona discovers there is a secret connected with the death of Jermyn's wife, Melanie, and that Jermyn himself is cold and forbidding. Before long, Anona finds herself falling in love with a man who tells her he can never return her love, and on the exotic island she finds both mystery and despair.